THAT'S BADD...

Intriguing Tales of a Small Market Town

Ann Elliott

Copyright © 2017 Ann Thornton Elliott
Doubletoil Press
All rights reserved.

ISBN-13:
978-1539963660

ISBN-10:
1539963667

That's Little Baddenham is a work of fiction. The names, characters, places, events and incidents portrayed are either products of the author's imagination or used in a fictitious manner. Any resemblance to actual persons, living or dead, or events, is purely co-incidental.

ACKNOWLEDGEMENTS

Thanks to:
W Flemming for cover pen-drawings
Adam Bealing for cover design
Helen Acton and David Ransome for advice on Suffolk dialect
Margherita Baker for proof reading
Leiston Writers, mostly pithy poets, for their support and advice.
Myself for interior design

Foreword

The creation and subject matter of many of these stories pre-date the age of universal internet and mobile phone use that has changed communication and fiction forever. What if Tess of the D'Urbeville's had been able to text Angel Clare on the night before their wedding? What if Romeo had received Friar Lawrence's letter about Juliet's apparent death? Countless plots depend on the miscarriage of vital information.

The fictional town of Little Baddenham and its environs is not unlike Framlingham, a small market town in East Suffolk, where I have lived for around twenty years. Yet it is not Framlingham — people familiar with the area will no doubt delight in noting the similarities and differences. Nor are the residents based on real people, but their troubles, loves, lives, idiosyncrasies, follies and vices are typical of those who live in such a town. A few stories contain a suggestion of Suffolk dialect as behoves their protagonists.

The five *Cruickshank Chronicles* are snapshots of family members' lives over several decades, rather than a mini family saga. Each stands alone and should be read where it comes in the overall sequence of thematically linked stories.

The stages of life in the collection range from early childhood through to old age, but not necessarily in chronological order.

The eighteenth century pioneer novelist, Henry Fielding, like Dickens after him, used punning names to shortcut meaning. Hence, there's 'little bad in them' — the inhabitants of Little Baddenham.

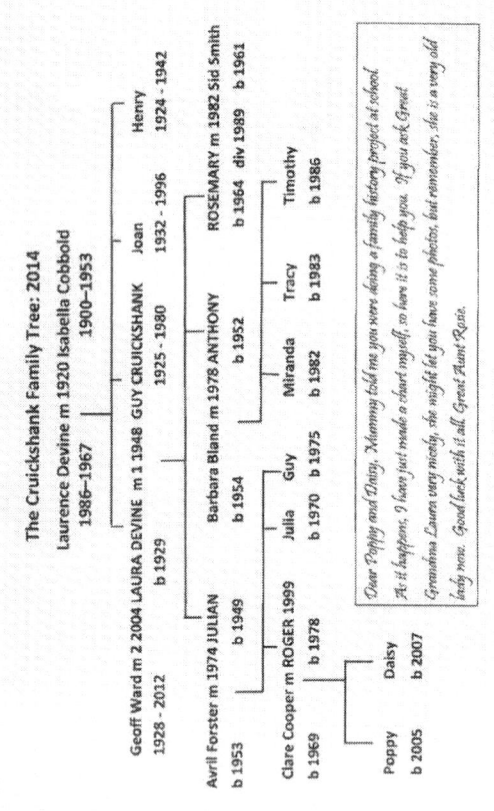

The Cruickshank Family Tree: 2014

Laurence Devine m 1920 Isabella Cobbold
1886–1967   1900–1953

Geoff Ward m 2 2004 LAURA DEVINE m 1 1948 GUY CRUICKSHANK   Joan   Henry
1928 - 2012   b 1929   1925 - 1980   1932 - 1996 1924 - 1942

Barbara Bland m 1978 ANTHONY   ROSEMARY m 1982 Sid Smith
                     b 1952   b 1964 div 1989 b 1961

Avril Forster m 1974 JULIAN   Julia   Guy   Miranda   Tracy   Timothy
b 1953   b 1949   b 1970   b 1975   b 1982   b 1983   b 1986

Clare Cooper m ROGER 1999
b 1969   b 1978

Poppy   Daisy
b 2005   b 2007

Dear Poppy and Daisy, Mummy told me you were doing a family history project at school. As it happens, I have just made a chart myself, so here it is to help you. If you ask Great Grandma Laura very nicely, she might let you have some photos, but remember, she is a very old lady now. Good luck with it all. Great Aunt Rosie.

CONTENTS

1	The Cruickshank Chronicles I	1
	Rites of Passage	
2	A Cautionary Tale	11
3	A Very Short Tail	21
4	Sickness Benefit	23
5	Scouting is for Boys	27
6	Scout's Honour	31
7	Charlie's Dead	41
8	Love Divine, All Loves Excelling	45
9	Where There's Hope	53
10	The Cruickshank Chronicles II	61
	All That Glisters is not Gold	
11	A Long Wait	71
12	Over the Top	77
13	The Eternal Quadrangle I	87
	Love, Love me, do	
14	The Norfolk Canary	95
15	There's None so Deaf	99
16	No Second Fiddle	113

17	A Tooth for a Tooth	121
18	The Cruickshank Chronicles III Rambling Rosie	129
19	Ill-considered Trifles	137
20	Great–I don't know how many times Great– Aunt Lizzie's Wedding Gown	149
21	Time and Time Again	157
22	The Other Side	167
23	Off of the Shelf	175
24	Grandfather Strikes Again	181
25	The Cruickshank Chronicles 1V The Thread of Life	185
26	A Case of Foul Play	191
27	The Eternal Quadrangle II Save All My Kisses	199
28	The Happening	215
29	The Copper Beech	221
30	The Cruickshank Chronicles V A Grave Mistake	227

THE CRUICKSHANK CHRONICLES I
RITES OF PASSAGE

It was done and there was no going back on it. The last guest was gone; the empty champagne bottles and sad remains of canapés cleared away; the Waterford flutes hand washed up and returned to the display cabinet. Laura was stretched out on a lounger in the orchard sipping the final dregs from dis-carded glasses. She glanced affectionately towards the rambling Georgian house.

Had they done the right thing?

Half smiling, she recalled her wedding day. Her stepmother, of course, had insisted on a church wedding, though Laura, having sloughed off organised religion in deference to her fiancé's outspoken atheism, would have preferred the registry office. At Sunday-School, Laura Devine and Guy Cruickshank had been sweethearts, and she had seen her young man off to the Second World War with trepidation. Her older brother Henry had been killed in action, but Guy had returned from France, avowing that there was no God.

Post-War austerity made it a simple affair, and the reception was held in the garden of Orchard Place, Laura's family home in the outskirts of little Baddenham. As they swept out of the drive in Guy's Alvis to honeymoon in Cromer, the gallant captain declared, in no uncertain terms, 'That's the last time you'll get me inside a church, living or dead.' And he'd kept to it, with the exception of attending the occasional concert, when he'd latterly been heard to say, 'Considering the excellent acoustic, St Edmund's would be a jolly good building for an Arts' Centre, if only they'd dump the mumbo-jumbo.'

Before they were married, Guy had begun adding to his inherited collection of Irish Waterford Crystal. As a surprise, Laura had presented him with a pair of multi-faceted champagne flutes, no expense spared for such an auspicious occasion. Guy was delighted. When it was time for the toasts, the champagne was poured, the happy couple raised their glasses, and Laura became gradually aware of a wetness on her wedding dress. She tore her eyes away from her new husband's gaze and looked down: precious liquid was leaking out of a hole in the side of the glass. On subsequent examination, it transpired there was a fault in the cutting.

'There's no point crying over spilt champagne, old girl,' guffawed Guy, and so they made light of it, laughing along with the assembled friends and relations.

Perhaps the ability to live and let live was the secret behind their thirty-odd successful years of marriage, not forgetting the two fine boys and Rosie, the afterthought.

Guy had toyed with several professions after leaving the army, and had eventually found himself happily trading in antiques in a barn on the estate. He and Laura shared the delights of horticulture and their attachment to Little Baddenham, the picturesque small market town in Suffolk, where they had lived most of their lives.

And now he was gone. Poor Guy, to have died so young seemed so unfair, but throat cancer is no respecter of age or a comparatively blameless life. When he'd been diagnosed, they had, naturally, revised their wills. Julian, their eldest son, a barrister, had seen to that. But in those last few days, when he'd barely been able to croak, he'd written a letter of wishes in collusion with the attendant District Nurse. It had dumfounded them all.

'I wish,' he had scrawled in straggling felt-tip script, 'that my body should be laid to repose in the orchard of Orchard Place where I have spent so many happy hours with my wife and family. I do not believe in God, nor that my body shall be translated into another dimension, so there will be no prayers, no clergy, no undertakers, no ceremony at all beyond my friends and family giving me a good send-off in the garden, weather permitting, of our home. I no longer wish my organs to be available for research or transplant, but I want my body to be buried whole, not cremated to dust and ashes, under the pear tree. This is my dying wish.' The signature was bold and clear.

*****

After her sons, Julian and Anthony, had left home, in spite of her husband's flippant protestations, Laura had taken to attending St Edmund's, at first spasmodically, then more regularly. Little Rosie had, if briefly, joined the choir.

The church had been so supportive during Guy's illness. When he died, the Vicar called to offer his services and condolences, several undertakers solicited her custom, and the boys and their wives gathered to discuss what best to do. Laura was in turmoil. Her religious self urged a conventional service; her wifely self urged compliance with her husband's wishes. Julian was worried about garden burial being in breach of the law; his wife Avril, who had once worked for the NHS, was worried about health and safety; Anthony, the accountant, was a bit squeamish at the idea and his wife Barbara, who was fanatical about cleanliness if not godliness, was outraged. Even Laura was concerned about What People Would Think. Poor Laura grew tired of the 'But Mothers' that blasted her from all sides.

'If it is acceptable to bury a cat or a dog in the garden, why not a man?' persisted Laura. She pictured herself down the years communing with her own true love in their private haven. Only Rosemary, overflowing with teenage sensibilities, was enchanted, and went around singing snatches of The Unquiet Grave. 'I'll never have but one true love, and in Green Wood he lies slain…'

And so it came to pass, exactly as Guy had wished, and he was laid to rest under his favourite pear tree. The boys sweated blood and tears digging the six foot hole, carefully reserving the turf, weeds and all, while their wives threw wobblies.

'We Cruickshanks have always been well respected,' pontificated Julian. 'Any hint of eccentricity would inevitably damage our reputation.'

In the interests of secrecy, the family finally agreed that they drop hints, to appropriate persons, that there had been a private, family only, cremation, and that the toasts at the wake were to Guy's ashes scattered under the pear tree. When their cleaner assumed this to be the case, they didn't disillusion her, thus avoiding outright duplicity. It was Avril, Julian's bosomy, braying wife, who suggested strewing cat litter over the hastily re-turfed grave to add verisimilitude.

Laura suffered agonies over the dishonesty, but at least she was spared the gossip and hostility of the good townsfolk of Little Baddenham who would undoubtedly be scandalised were the truth to be known—rumour was one of their favourite pursuits. Even forthright Barbara, a ticking time-bomb, managed to hold her peace.

After the funeral kerfuffle was over, Laura planted a bed of all Guy's favourite flowers and shrubs over the grave: honesty, love-in-the-mist, forget-me-nots, pansies, aromatic lavender and rosemary. Overlooking the spot, she built a pergola with sweet-scented honeysuckle and rambling roses. She revelled in sitting there, sharing her views and news with the dearly departed.

*****

It wasn't long before the boys, their wives, their children, her friends, even the Vicar, urged Laura to downsize. Over the years, she shrugged off their advice.

'Orchard Place is much too big for you, now you're on your own,' Avril would advise. True, but she loved it.

'Keeping up an old house like this costs a fortune,' Anthony would say. So it did, but in spite of inflation, she could get by as her wants were simple. She was almost self-sufficient, employing a part-time gardener to grow vegetables and help with the hens who scratched away in the orchard. Lacking Guy's expertise, she sold his antique business and received a substantial rent for the barn from the new dealer.

'Think what you'd save if you moved into a smart little bungalow,' Barbara would plead. 'It would be maintenance-free and so easy to keep clean, not like this old wreck. You could afford to travel.'

'It's all very well Rosemary taking herself off for years and disappearing with hardly a trace, but I have no desire to travel. I'm happy here with my memories like my parents and grandparents before me.'

*****

Laura held out until she was seventy-one when she'd been briefly hospitalised by a stupid fall, and her 'treasure', Norma, deserted her to become a care assistant. Besides, as the years passed, the thoughts of the things the family ought not to have done were increasingly preying on her mind and she was no longer comfortable sitting under the pear tree. So, she gave in gracefully and looked for a suitable bungalow, not too close to her son Julian, in Great Baddenham.

As for Orchard Place, the boys had it freshened up a bit before putting it on the market.

> *Desirable residence in need of refurbishment with huge potential for a variety of uses. Grade 2 listed, Georgian fronted, many period features, 8 bedrooms, 4 reception rooms, extensive grounds and a range of outbuildings ...*

'What if new owners re-lay the garden and come across Pop's bones?' said Anthony.

'It doesn't bear thinking of,' said Avril.

'Let's lay a new patio over the grave,' said Julian. 'If we use recycled paving slabs no-one will know it hasn't been there since the year dot. Best let sleeping bones lie.'

Being somewhat dilapidated and with a hefty asking price, Orchard Place was on the market for so long that, having settled on a sparkling new bungalow, spacious but with a compact garden, Laura moved in without hanging on for the sale. Rosemary had turned up out of the blue yonder soon after the For Sale signs had gone up and it was such a comfort to know she'd be keeping a family toe in the old place.

*****

The church in Great Baddenham was very active and Laura soon made friends.

'I don't know what's possessed you Mother,' pronounced Anthony when Laura introduced him to a recently widowed church stalwart of a suitable age who had prevailed upon her to change her name for his own.

'Marriage at your age, it's ridiculous,' said Julian. 'You must make a new will, you know.'

'If it's your inheritance you're worried about, you needn't—Geoffrey doesn't need my money and I love him.'

Only Rosie was enchanted.

'You'll be able to have that posh church wedding you dreamt of as a girl, Ma, with a bevy of granddaughters in attendance.'

*****

Eventually, a couple with a large family fell in love with Orchard Place and bought it. Just before completion, Laura felt the urge to show her new fiancé her old haunts. The house, bereft of furniture, the walls patterned with pale rectangles where pictures had hung, the creaking floorboards, still held faint resonances of the laughing years. Only the kitchen, with its venerable fittings, retained its ambience. For occasional visits, the old deal table and a couple of worm-ridden chairs remained.

'Sit down, Geoff, I've brought a flask.' They drank coffee comfortably while Laura regaled him with family anecdotes. Geoff, being tidy minded, then insisted on hacking back the ivy that was inveigling itself through the window frame. 'Do you mind if I go outside to say goodbye to the garden while you finish?'

Laura kissed him lightly, slipped out through the back door and, forging a track through with her walking stick, wound her way along unkempt paths to the orchard. Should, or should she not, confess her guilty secret? That, against the law, against health and safety regulations, against common decency, they had buried her husband right there in the orchard. Perhaps Guy would advise her. She'd half forgotten that the boys had laid that silly patio. The whole area was sadly overgrown, the honeysuckle and climbing roses rampant round the pergola. 'Rambling Rosie', she noted, was surviving the neglect. She bashed the nettles aside so she could sit down. The perfume was glorious, the birds still sang.

'Guy, it's me Laura, I know it's been a while… I just wanted your blessing on Geoff and me. It's not that I'll ever stop loving you Guy… And those sons of yours have been so difficult, all that business about your bones… I hated the dishonesty, I felt so guilty…'

Guy's presence was faint, fading... Laura experienced a moment of wild panic. Perhaps he disapproved…

'Should I fess up Guy?'

But his image was receding as a swishing of undergrowth heralded Geoff's arrival.

A Cautionary Tale

My old friend Caroline had been talking of visiting me for years, but somehow it had never happened. 'Furthest Suffolk isn't exactly on the way to anywhere,' she would say. She and her husband were keen motor caravanners, and undertook lengthy pilgrimages. I must say, she had a point, and chose to ignore the implication that I wasn't worth visiting in my own right.

Now, Little Baddenham is frequently extolled in quality newspapers as being one of the best places to live in Suffolk, East Anglia, the entire UK, or even the world. The articles and surveys dwell on the town's unique qualities; its old world charm; its convenience for the coast; its beautiful countryside; its independent shops; the friendliness of the inhabitants; its fine craft centre; the heritage landmarks—the fine Norman Castle and the magnificent medieval St Edmund's Church.

After one such panegyric, Caroline emailed me: 'are you free to be visited next weekend? Phil is away at a conference…'

Because of a traffic-delaying accident on the A14, she didn't arrive till late Friday evening. Rufus, my geriatric toy-poodle, greeted her with his usual twirly-whirly routine. She declined my offer of a meal, but I brought out nibbles and red wine. We sat on the sofa with the dog blissfully lap-switching and demanding titbits.

'Is Little Baddenham as idyllic as they make out, Annabel?' she asked when we'd caught up on our lives and reminisced about our student days.

'It is, and it isn't. It's pretty well autonomous. Some people are snobby about Alldays, the local supermarket, and insist on driving into Great Baddenham Tesco's, but we can buy pretty well anything here. We have excellent schools, churches, medical facilities, if you need something fixing, there's someone to fix it.

'That's all very well, but being so isolated, isn't it a cultural desert?'

'No way! There's always something on, cultural, sporting, or social. There are concerts in the church, plays at the college theatre, film club, art club, choral society, literary groups, bridge, the list is endless. People flock from miles around for the Gala, pronounced 'Gayla' would you believe! Little Baddenham isn't chocolate-boxy like Lavenham, nor posh like Aldeburgh. We encourage tourists— English Heritage stages historical re-creations. We have an over-abundance of eateries, but we refuse to flood the town with antique and giffte shoppes, so it retains its flavour as a working market town, though lots of people commute now, alas.'

'What's the down side then?'

'There' a huge lobby against massive housing developments that threaten to ruin the ambience of the town. Parking is a pain, and the medieval streets weren't designed for juggernauts or two-way traffic. We're miles from big main roads and trains, but that's no bad thing, it keeps us self-sufficient. Like pre-TV times, we have to make our own entertainment. And, although people complain, you can get by on buses, just about. More plonk?'

My sofa is all of two feet from the pavement outside. Every so often, we were disturbed by the Friday-night youth rampaging up and down: harsh adolescent male voices, shouting, swearing, bouncing gun-fire footballs; girls, shrieking and no doubt displaying their thighs provocatively.

'Where on earth are they going?' Caroline looked askance.

'I've no idea, the sports' club, the skate-park perhaps, or to each other's houses. All testosterone and nowhere to go. There's little bad in them, though I confess I find them mildly intimidating, even if it's only youthful high spirits.'

I was just pouring the last of the red wine when there was a hammering on the window, so thunderous that we all but jumped out of our skins. Poor old Rufus, who is almost stone deaf, leaped up to see it off.

Manic barking.

'That's outrageous,' said Caroline, who lives in a cul-de-sac. She was half way to the door, phone in hand, to capture the culprits on camera.

'Leave them be, Caroline. There's no point antagonising them, and no harm's done.'

'But that was so scary, I dread to think what it would do to some frail old person with a heart condition.'

It was only then that I noticed a pool of red wine sloshed onto the carpet.

'Oh bugger,' I said. 'Was it the bomb-blast or the dog that made me spill the plonk?'

*****

After a lazy breakfast, we made a couple of circuits of the Castle Meadow, where every other person has a dog, or dogs, who yap or gambol about, or chase after balls, or inspect each other's rear ends, while the owners pass on the gossip of the day.

'Walking a dog is such a good way of making friends. Rufus, stop eating that rabbit poo… Hi Marion. Hi Sandy.'

'Darcy, do you have to roll in that fox dirt. Darce!' But he'd chased off after Marion's miniature schnauzer, his next best friend. Rufus set off to follow, but stopped in his tracks, looking round forlornly. Poor old boy is nearly blind. I clapped, made hand signals, but he looked over the expanse of green sward, beyond the dry moat, towards the cobbled castle wall, pricking his ears for the echo of my voice. Realising he'd lost me, he stood still, in spite of being practically bowled over by Rags and Rover, the big dog brigade. I clapped again, but Rufus set off towards a total stranger.

'There's fidelity—any Mum will do!' said Sandy. 'Hi Stella.'

Stella's Georgie was busy eating something at the top of the field and wouldn't be dissuaded.

'He's got a myxie rabbit,' shouted Stella. 'Ugh. I can't bear those protruding eyes. Hi Rosie! Don't let Percy off…'

Caroline and I got within clap-shot of Rufus, put him on his lead, clicked the gate shut, leaving the big dogs to it.

A couple of helmeted cyclists, visitors perhaps, or perhaps not, were racing past the church in the wrong direction.

'Excuse me,' I said, not impolitely, 'do you know that this is a one-way street?' They ignored me and careered on down the hill.

'It's OK if you want to kill yourselves,' I shouted after them, 'but it's not fair on the other people. Cars zoom round that corner and they're not expecting oncoming traffic.'

'Well done you,' said Caroline. 'People are so thoughtless.'

'At least they didn't give me any lip! They think they're invulnerable.'

'But it's not only the youngsters, Annabel…'

'Like parking on double yellow lines. They think the rules don't apply to them.'

'Hark at us! Anyone would take us for our mothers.'

'Or our grandmothers!'

We sauntered on to the Market Hill, waving and greeting acquaintances, for everyone knows everybody else in Little Baddenham.

Or at least some of them.

The town buzzes on a summer Saturday morning. The market bustles with shoppers, small children, buggies, dogs, pensioners, or tourists. A solitary saxophonist or guitarist serenades the town centre.

Enticing smells assault the taste-buds: fresh fish, cheese and pies; artisan bread and pastries; gloriously coloured fruit and veg; cut flowers, plants. The most colourful display is the ethnic woven-basket and hat stall. There is a caravan coffee-shop, another with home-reared meat busy barbecuing sausages, burgers and pulled pork. Sometimes there are craft stalls or charity stalls...

'Morning Alice,' I said to a flamboyantly draped old biddy sitting behind a junk-posing-as-antique stall.

Some well-mannered teenagers from the High School were touting their wares, some business start-up project to nurture good citizens of the future.

'The town indulges in ritual coffee-drinking on Saturdays,' I said, indicating sprawling bistro furniture on the wide pavements. 'The Dancing Goat is my favourite, but my friends prefer The Crown.'

I ushered Caroline through the hotel lounge, black beams, scrubbed deal tables. Rufus was pulling to greet his friend, a pretty little King Charles spaniel.

'There's a lovely courtyard at the back if it's warm enough. Fido's mum had a heart condition and was failing for years before she died. She spoilt that dog rotten, gave him tea and bacon and egg for breakfast.' I waved at my friends who were already sitting under a parasol.

'I hope she didn't die of fright then from someone bashing her window,' Caroline was saying as we approached the table.

'No, she had a heart-attack and fell—Fido alerted the neighbours, so sad.' I introduced Pat, Marion,

Mary and Gwen. We made much, as ever, of ordering our drinks.

'So you had them banging on your widow too Annabel?' said Pat. 'It sounded like a terrorist attack! Is your wing mirror OK? Mine was snapped back, and so was my neighbour's.'

'It takes me for ever to realign it once it's been knocked,' said Gwen.

'It can be an accident, like if you have to squeeze between two badly parked cars,' I added.

'Or if you have a near miss,' put in Pat.

'But to do it on purpose, it's not only criminal but dangerous,' I protested virulently.

'Calm down Annabel, for heaven's sake,' said Caroline. 'Rufus, stop licking my leg.'

'But surely, everyone checks their mirrors automatically before driving off? That's what I was taught,' said Mary.

'I always do, but what if you forget?' said Gwen. 'We're all getting a bit forgetful…'

'I remember reading about an accident in my local paper,' chipped in Caroline.

We were all agog.

'There was a medical emergency. A fall from the climbing frame was it? Anyway, the father dialled 111, then 999. When no-one turned up, he bundled the little boy into the back seat of his car and rushed to the hospital himself. He failed to see a car coming out of a slipway and pulled over. The coroner concluded the nearside mirror was out of alignment.'

We fell silent.

Briefly.

'D'you mean someone was killed?' said Gwen.

'Yes, the little boy. The father survived—his airbags kicked in. Both cars were a right-off, and it was touch-and-go for the other driver. What's more, the father insisted the mirrors were OK—he'd adjusted them before leaving the office the evening before and hadn't used the car since. So it's likely it was deliberate vandalism.'

'What a thing for him to have to live with,' said Pat.

'Did they find the culprits?' asked Gwen.

'The police visited the schools and lectured the kids on the need for responsible behaviour and anticipating the consequences of their actions, but no-one owned up.'

'These young people are so inconsiderate,' said Marion. 'We never behaved like that…'

'It's not that they're vicious, they just don't think,' said Pat.

Having thus put the world to rights, people started making a move. I untangled Rufus, who had been playing maypoles with the chair leg.

Caroline and I headed for the church, up the time-worn steps.

'It's good to think of so many generations of feet hollowing out the stone on their way to services,' said Caroline.

'True, but with an ageing population, it could be dangerous for anyone that's unsteady on their feet.'

Light was streaming through the art-deco window panes, making crisscross patterns on the flagstones. A church warden was pointing visitors toward information boards, the famous organ, the renaissance tombs of the mighty. Flower arrangers were gossiping in undertones. Rufus, as ever, stalled at the metal grills on the floor.

'He thinks there are dragons down there,' I smiled indulgently.

'Beowulf's dragon, perhaps.'

'Oh, I nearly forgot. Look, at the carvings on the font, it's the martyrdom of St Edmund.'

'There he is, stuck full of Viking arrows.'

'Like a hedgehog!' we chorused, recalling our Anglo-Saxon studies.

'And just look at the Wolf guarding the kingly head, even though he was ravenous.'

'What a wonderful building,' said Caroline.

'Yes, we're very lucky. But it's seldom peaceful in here, there's always someone coming and going.'

The day was still glorious as we sat outside the Dancing Goat with paninis and smoothies, watched the world go by.

'Don't you think Little Baddenham's archetypally English?' I said, savouring the last bite.

'Since you're waxing lyrical, what about Old John of Gaunt's speech in Henry V?'

We broke into a chant, ending with:

'This blessed plot, this earth, this realm, this England...'

*****

I felt at a bit of a loose end after Caroline had left, relaxed with Sunday night comfort-zone TV, finished the dregs of the wine, watched Look East, not much news at the weekend…

Then there was a news flash: 'There has been pile up on the A14, an elderly woman is reported dead and several people were taken to hospital in a serious condition…'

A VERY SHORT TAIL

'It's a springer spaniel!' says a voice, savouring the words with the absolute assurance of say three-and-three-quarters tomorrow. 'It's a springer spaniel.'

'I think it's a poodle,' says Mummy.

'No, it's a springer spaniel. Silly!'

'Yes it's a poodle,' I say, turning round. The boy is all eyes, half running to keep up with the buggy. 'Poodles come in three sizes. This high, and this high and this high. Tall, smaller, smallest. The smallest is called a toy poodle.' Rufus is busy stretching up to wash the sticky hand in the buggy.

'Oh.' Puzzled

'Rufus isn't a puppy. He's as old as your grandad. He won't grow any taller. He's a toy poodle.'

'Oh!' We all pace along. 'Is he real?' Mummy and I try to muffle our laughter.

'Of course he's real.'

'Has he got wheels?' hoots the child. The grey, draggled toy doggie with one shining eye drifts up from my childhood, with, alas, no tail to wag, much like Rufus, who was docked by his breeder. Mummy and I and the baby chortle out loud.

'No he hasn't got wheels. He's real. You can stroke him if you like.'

The child strokes Rufus, who gets on his hind legs to lick him.

'He's got wheels,' crows the child delightedly.

'Oh no he hasn't!'

'Oh yes he has.'

'Oh no he hasn't!' Rufus pauses on the clump of weeds beside the Con Club Wall and cocks his leg. 'Look, he's having a wee. That proves he's real!'

We cross the road and turn through the kissing gate at the top of the footpath and splash through the puddle.

'It's a poodle,' I hear, retreating. 'It's a poodle!' crows the child with the absolute assurance of say three-and-three-quarters tomorrow.

Sickness Benefit

Harry and Grandad were in the park throwing sticks for Sam the Collie, when they noticed the garish poster on the dog's favourite lamp post. 'Fred's Fantastic Funfair' it blazed. 'Gala Weekend.'

'Wow!' was their spontaneous reaction.

'Mum and Dad will never let us go. It's not fair. Everyone else at school will be going and I'll feel such a wimp… '

'When I were ten, we could go anywhere, run around in the streets all day, and none of this talk of nowhere being safe for children. Or old men, come to think. Them were the days! Mind you, my dad he give us a clip round the ear or worse if we stepped out of line.' Sam head-butted Harry for his lead.

'Couldn't *you* take me Grandad?'

'I'd never hear the last of it from your Mum if I did. Sorry Harry.'

'But what if she didn't know?'

'She'd be bound to find out. She's got a fine long pair of ears, your Mum.' Harry hadn't noticed Mum's ears being longer than other people's.

Sometimes Grown-ups said really silly things. Perhaps this was one of them.

'Mum's such a spoilsport,' Harry seethed. 'If only they were ill, you could take me.' Grandad's eyes gleamed.

'We'll see.' And they went to the allotment to dig potatoes. Sam scrabbled under the red-veined leaves of the rhubarb clump in search of an old ball.

'Don't touch them leaves, boy, them's poisonous.' Grandad scratched his head thoughtfully.

The morning of the Gala arrived. Harry had lain awake half the night dreaming of the bright lights, the rides, the prizes, as the whole town throbbed with the sounds of the machinery and music. On Friday nights, Harry's mum dragged him to Alldays for the weekly shop. Harry hated supermarkets, but for once, he didn't itch to join his friends in circuit-training round the aisles as his mind struggled with the quagmire of schemes.

He enjoyed feeding the pound coin into the trolley slot — Mum sometimes let him keep it at the end if she was in a good mood. He even offered to push the trolley, and was unaccountably let off the usual warning. Grandad had been most specific, but surely Mum would suspect… At last, the chill of the fruit and veg aisle. Harry screeched the trolley to a halt beside the pre-packed salads, his eyes on stalks. He'd hide one away if need be.

'Baby leaves, that looks nice,' he suggested.

'Pardon? You hate salad! 'Spinach, beetroot leaves, rocket…'

'Rocket? Wow.' Into the trolley went the pack. Mission accomplished, but would it work? The glorious picture of him and Grandad on the Big Wheel spurred him on.

'Mind you don't eat that greenery,' Grandad hissed as they sat down to lunch. 'At least not the reddish bits. I've doctored it like we said,' Grandad winked.

Harry fretted about what he'd say if Mum told him off for not eating all the salad he'd made such a fuss about buying.

Later, Mum and Dad both complained of stomach cramps, and obligingly took to their bed, amid frequent flushings of the lavatory.

At dusk, Harry and Grandad sneaked out. The joys of the funfair surpassed all their expectations. Harry went quiet as they neared home, cluttered with hard-earned prizes. There was a cold knot in the pit of his stomach.

'They won't die, will they?'

'Course not! You'd need pounds of rhubarb leaves for that!' Harry relaxed. 'But your Uncle Simon, he died, falling off of a ride, about your age he was, boy. So don't be too hard on your mum. She were hully upset, losing her only brother like that, she's never really recovered. And she's only anxious for your own good.'

Sam barked rapturously as the key turned, jumped up as they came into the hall, scattering the trophies.

'Is that you Grandad?' came a feeble voice from upstairs. Harry stopped in his tracks, torn between relief and fear of detection.

'We could murder a cup of tea!'

SCOUTING IS FOR BOYS

Jennifer was playing houses under the dining room table. She was giving Teddy and Jumbo their tea in honour of the new tea-set with shiny red and green knives that nearly cut. It was a bit like being in a dark forest, the way the mossy cloth hung down. She sawed at a biscuit saved from her own meal, holding her breath in case Michael heard it crack. Michael was swinging his legs dangerously at one end of the table and making concentrating noises. 'Come out of there you silly little squirt,' he'd say if he found out she was there. She hated Michael, though when she was little, she'd actually wanted to marry him! How foolish she'd been. Nowadays, he never wanted to play with her at all, and was always teasing her when Mummy and Daddy weren't there. And they'd laughed out loud when she'd put 'my big bother' in her composition at school. And they'd given him a smart blue bike for passing his eleven plus, and now he'd joined the Scouts.

'Mummy, can you please test me on the Scout Law?' Jennifer lay on her tummy and saw Mummy bustling in, pulling down her sleeves from the washing up. Mummy winked and sat down at the table with the book in front of her.

'Fire away then.'

'A Scout...' Jennifer mouthed it all to Teddy and Jumbo. 'A Scout smiles and whistles under all difficulties.'

A sort of snort came from Daddy's arm-chair. 'I'd like to see him try!'

Michael didn't hear and went on chanting. Jennifer tried it. She couldn't actually whistle yet, but she knew you had to screw your mouth up tight, and when she tried to smile, it sounded like when Michael let down the tyres on her fairy bike. Michael's feet stopped dangling, and he stood up straight, with one grey sock flopping round his ankle.

'I promise to do my best, to do my duty to God and the King and to obey the Scout Law.'

'Queen!' yelled Jennifer, forgetting she was in hiding. She crawled out, and stood there indignantly, arms akimbo. 'It's the Queen now. Brown Owl said.'

'My goodness, what a surprise!' and Mummy hustled her off to bed. She turned at the door to stick her tongue out at Michael. Later, snuggled up with Teddy and Jumbo, she grew very worried indeed. How could Michael possibly stand up in front of everyone and promise to smile and whistle at the same time when it was an impossible feat?

'Have you got into bed yet?' called her mother the next night, and the next.

'I haven't finished brushing my teeth.'

This wasn't a lie, since she'd spent ages in front of the bathroom mirror vainly trying to force her mouth into a smiling, whistling sort of shape.

At the end of Brownies, Jennifer helped with the clearing up.

'Brown Owl, can I ask you something?' Brown Owl was the Vicar's wife, she'd be bound to know.

'Of course dear.' She went on counting the skipping ropes.

'You know when you make a solemn promise? You have to mean it don't you?'

'Of course you do dear. It would by lying to make a promise if you didn't intend to keep it and telling lies is always wrong.'

'But what if you thought you meant the promise because you didn't know you couldn't possibly keep it?'

'Well that would depend... Ah here's the caretaker to lock up. Why don't you come and talk it over with the Vicar dear?'

Jennifer didn't like the Reverend Power. He had whiskers and a red face and smelt of carbolic soap. Besides, he might say that Michael would end up in hell.

Jennifer tried to warn Michael of the peril he was in, but he wouldn't listen and kept on pulling her pigtails and calling her names. Perhaps she could get Daddy to tell him, but he wasn't much help.

'If the great Baden Powell laid down the Scout Law, then I should say it's all right.'

Afterwards, she wondered if Daddy had been being sarcastic. And she'd been going to get him to write to BP.

The day of Michael's enrolment came.

'Liar,' she hissed, when he returned to show off his badge, and at every subsequent opportunity.

*****

Jennifer did her best to be a good Brownie. She yearned for a red bike and to fly up to 1st Little Baddenham Guides. She passed her eleven plus and got the red bike, but when Brown Owl asked her about ordering her Guide uniform, she tearfully replied:

'I'm *not* going to Guides. It would be hypocritical,' and cycled off at full speed.

In September, her friends began swotting up the Guide Law, not always in the dinner hour.

'Go on Jen, test us.' She bristled and scowled. 'It's all lies.' But she couldn't help overhearing them.

'A Guide smiles and sings under all difficulties.' She couldn't believe her ears and grabbed the book. There it was, in black and white. 'Sings' not 'whistles'. Miss Murdoch was constantly telling the school choir to smile while they sang.

She cycled home, smiling and singing all the way, to tell Mummy to order her Guide uniform. She even smiled and sang at Michael, who'd now outgrown Scouts.

Scout's Honour

Chris had never wanted to go to Scout Camp, but for once, his father had over-ruled Mummy and that was that.

'Weak chest, weak eyesight my eye,' grumbled Daddy. 'Do you want to make a milksop of him?'

'But the weather's been so awful. That Norfolk coast can be quite chilly. He's bound to catch cold.'

'Peter will keep an eye on him, he's his Patrol Leader.'

If only they knew! He'd never told yet of his cousin's unremitting bullying.

*****

Chris was sitting, huddled miserably in the shelter of a hedge, anxiously peering through the leaves to where Hawk Patrol was cooking breakfast. He shivered as the smell of frying bacon tortured the empty pit of his stomach. Whenever a puff of wood smoke swirled his way, his tired eyes smarted dreadfully and he was getting a bit tight-chested, but Skip had his inhaler. How could he possibly regain camp without being seen? Skip was giving the Hawks the benefit of his experience and he daren't risk being spotted escaping the hedge. 'No one must ever know,' Poisonous Pete had decreed.

Last night had been the worst ordeal of his life. It was nearly Lights Out when he got back to the big bell tent. Opening the flap, he saw a nightlight flickering over the circle of shadowy faces. Suddenly, his eye-balls were assailed by a merciless beam of light. Pete's voice spat out from behind the glare.

'Constipated again Chrissy?' Chris writhed at the humiliation.

'We've got some tests for you. Just to prove you're One of Us.' Chris could feel five pairs of eyes boring into him, his hands were pinioned. 'Drink this,' came Pete's voice. 'Dandelion tea, prepared by my own fair hand.' Chris choked and tried to spit out the noxious brew. The voice turned into a hiss, and the hiss was taken up by the others in a ritual chant.

'Sissy Chrissy, Piss-the-bed Chris. Sissy Chrissy, Piss-the-bed Chris.'

'OK Kestrels, it's time you stopped messing around.' Skip's voice boomed from just outside the tent. The searchlight blanked out and everyone froze. Chris felt his chest tighten. *Please not an asthma attack.* But Skip didn't intervene. 'And don't let me catch you with a lantern on after Lights Out again, or you might just find yourselves losing that Mascot Hat. I'd have thought better of you, Pete.'

'I'm sorry Skip. It won't happen again. I didn't realise it was so late, Scout's Honour!'

Why could no-one see through Pete's wily ways?

'Good night.'

'Good Night Skip.' As the footsteps squelched away, the patrol relaxed.

'Thought you'd got away with it did you, Chrissy?'

'Don't be so stupid Pete, you heard what Skip said.' *No one else would stick up for him.*

'So I'm stupid, am I? Just you wait and see what happens to boys guilty of insubordination, family or no family!'

Chris strove to force back tears of indignation. *At least they wouldn't see.*

'If you want to redeem yourself, you'll obey my orders. Totally. Agreed guys?' Pete swung his beam round the ring of faces.

'Anything you say.'

'At my command, you get out and stay out till breakfast. No skulking in the marquee. No sucking up to the Scouters with excuses about your inhaler. If you tell anyone, ever, I'll hear about it, and I'll have your goolies for garters! OK?'

Chris nodded miserably. They circled round the tent-pole with Chris-in-the-middle while Pete administered a lengthy oath of obedience.

'I swear, Scout's Honour.' He'd just have to play along and prove he wasn't scared. Snoopy peeked through the tent flap.

'All clear,' he whispered, muffling a sneeze.

'And as a special privilege you can take the Mascot Hat. You might find one of BP's many uses for it.' Pete's hand yanked off Chris's glasses and roughly crushed the old-fashioned scout hat over his face. 'And guard it with your life! The honour of the Kestrels is at stake.'

Chris was thrust out into the night, alone, blind. He pushed up the hat and took great gulps of fresh air. 'And don't tread on your glasses. Here.' As he stooped and felt around until his fingers found them, his campfire blanket trailed wetly round his bare legs.

*****

It could have been worse. The dew was heavy, but at least the moon was full. The Scouters were laughing in the marquee, their shadows grotesquely distorted by the hurricane lamp.

'I'd swear Kestrel Patrol was up to something, but I left them to it.' Chris crept past, not daring to hear more. He'd noticed a hedge with a slightly sunken passage down the middle which would provide ideal cover. He pictured the old smugglers silently carrying home their casks of contraband brandy, in fear of the revenue men and their lives. If only it wasn't getting so cold, it might be quite fun. He'd just show Poisonous Peter... .

*****

The floor of the hedge snapped crackled and popped as he walked. At last, a dryish tree stump. Chris sat down, plonked the hat on his head and snuggled into his damp blanket.

He'd gained his Naturalist's Badge, so was more startled than frightened by the countless little rustlings of the creatures of the night. A family of rabbits was munching in the moonlight, then scattered, white scuts flying. A fox stood sniffing the wind, its neck stretched taut, then loped off with an unearthly cry. Chris nearly bit his tongue when an owl swept past his ear, screeching outlandishly. He watched, fascinated, as it glided over the hill.

*****

The hours dragged on. At last, the sky grew lighter. He'd never seen anything as beautiful as the sun creeping up from the horizon in a pink glow, splashing the fluffy clouds with a whole palette of colours. And the dawn chorus — his heart lurched at the joy of it — and he'd survived the rigours of the night! Perhaps he was outgrowing his asthma. Now it was all over, he couldn't wait to boast about it. Mummy would inevitably fuss, but Daddy might be proud of him. His heart sank — he was sworn to secrecy…

It sank more. How on earth could he break cover? The pale sun had transformed the gleaming whiteness of the field, the moon's hummocky mounds were fading, but some association of ideas produced inspiration. Flinging off his blanket, Mascot Hat in hand, he ran within the confines of the hedge right to the top of the dew-decked and gossamered field.

Half an hour later, he sauntered towards his patrol kitchen, the hat overflowing with freshly picked mushrooms. *Help, Skip was loitering around.*

'Food for free Sir!' Skip looked impressed. 'I remembered them from the hike.'

'That's very enterprising young Chris. BP would have approved! Well done!' Chris glowed with satisfaction. 'How about sharing your secret knowledge!'

He led a few scouts up the field.

'You're ace Chris, and we all thought you were a bit of a weed.' The comment was double-edged, but he didn't mind.

*****

Later, he noticed a huddle of boys bent double, eaves-dropping outside Skip's tent. Pete's voice rang out.

'I'm a bit worried about my young cousin, Skip. He hasn't been away from home before, and I think he's feeling homesick. In fact, to put it bluntly, he's been bed-wetting. Of course I've kept it to myself, but I thought you ought to know.' Surely Skip must hear the surge of stifled giggles through the thin canvass.

Chris blushed scarlet, the glory of his success gone, his confident walk disintegrating into a shamefaced shamble. He threw himself onto his sleeping bag. Ugh, it was damp and sticky. Now they'd all be calling him 'Piss-the bed-Chris!' Pete was a cunning devil. Supposing Skip got wind of Chris's all night ordeal, the wetness of the bed would allay his suspicions and Pete and his cronies would get away with it.

*****

Chris longed to go home to Little Baddenham, but that would be giving in. Pete despised him as a Mummy's boy, and even Daddy thought he was a drip. How could he be good at games, with his poor eyesight and asthma?

Bleary-eyed, Chris steeled himself to ignore the little titters and scornful glances. Tent Inspection was dire. They put their bedding out to air each morning, and he lost points for losing his campfire blanket.

Lefty didn't comment on the tell-tale wetness on his sleeping bag.

*****

'Anything wrong, Chris?' Skip appeared out of nowhere.

'No.'

'Are you sure?' Chris nodded, scarlet faced. 'You'd tell me if there was, wouldn't you?'

'Oh yes,' he lied, wondering if Pete was spying on the interview.

'Quite a lot of boys feel homesick on their first camp. It's nothing to be ashamed of.' Out of the corner of his eye, he could see Lefty gesticulating fiercely at Pete, who for once looked distinctly sheepish.

'But I'm not homesick Skip. Scout's Honour.'

*****

They stayed in camp that day, and made gadgets, complicated constructions of wood and string: bedding racks, billycan holders, towel airers. Chris, neat fingered and precise, enjoyed the challenge of making something out of nothing much, and his natty device for draining plates won great aplomb.

Most efforts collapsed when tested, amid gales of laughter.

Snoopy laughed so much the tears rolled down his face. Then suddenly he was breathless, wheezing great rattling gasps.

'Stop messing around you nerd,' snorted Pete. But Chris was already sitting Snoopy down and supporting his back.

'Now, keep calm, slow deep breaths. Has this happened before?' Grey-faced, Snoopy shook his head. *Why were they all standing there doing nothing?* 'Quick, someone fetch Skip—he'll need my inhaler. Call an ambulance.'

'Only a wimp like you could overreact like this Chris,' taunted Pete. 'Pull yourself together Snoopy.'

'He can't, he's having an acute asthma attack. Don't you understand? He can't breathe.' Seeing the panic in Snoopy's eyes, Chris winked desperately at Pete, who was faffing around like a headless chicken.

*****

Pete drew Chris aside at Camp Fire that night.

'I never thought you had it in you Chris, you've done really well. Sorry for being such a pig.'

*****

At Flag Break next morning, Skip assured them Snoopy was going to be all right.

'But if it wasn't for Chris Lambe's swift reaction, it might have been touch and go. Come here Chris. Blushing, he went forward and saluted. 'I don't think we can give you a Life Saver's Badge, but let's have a round of applause.'

When the cheering stopped, Skip continued.

'Thanks to Chris's ingenuity with gadgets, the Kestrels have again won the patrol trophy. Here Chris, please accept the Mascot Hat.' They all clapped.

*****

When he phoned home to his parents in Little Baddenham, Chris was able to fend off his mother's anxiety with:

'I'm fine. Scout's Honour.'

And he wasn't lying.

Charlie's Dead

Maggie was the one who was always picked last for the netball team. Her mother was older than everybody else's mother and only read magazines in the dentist's waiting room. She encouraged Maggie to be a swot, to despise Games and to drink the tepid free school milk that most girls left untouched in the crates in the dining hall. Getting the straw through the clotting top of the milk was quite a challenge.

When puberty declared itself, Maggie's mother produced a tinned-salmon coloured bra and sanitary belt she described as 'natural'. The advent of first bras was a significant topic among the whisperers in the post-gym communal shower room. All the other girls sported lily white bras. Maggie was too embarrassed to enlighten her mother and suffered in silence. Susanna Robinson was rumoured to take a size 36, at once derided, and aspired to.

The vagaries of school buses meant the pupils of Little Baddenham County Grammar School for Girls were destined seldom to cross paths with the boys from the College.

'You might as well be going in opposite directions on an escalator on the London Underground,' bemoaned Pauline Finch.

Maggie's mother had been jilted twice before marrying her father and pursed her lips whenever she noticed any of Maggie's friends holding hands with boys in the street. Maggie just thought it was soppy and continued to immerse herself in her studies.

Now Maggie had a Dutch pen-pal, her best friend Pauline likewise. The summer after O-levels, Pauline's dad bundled the girls onto the Harwich ferry and they were met by Anneke's family at Rotterdam and driven to Amsterdam. Anneke had two brothers, one a little squirt, but Henk was suave and handsome and Maggie enjoyed the first pangs of unrequited love.

The four girls had a fine old time, art galleries, a Chinese meal, the Amsterdam canals, and shopping in the *De Bijenkorf* department store. They flounced around the fitting rooms with cries of 'Charlie's dead' or 'de melk gekookt boven' when petticoats frothed beneath the shorter skirts. None of them knew the derivation of the English phrase but they chortled at the aptness of 'the milk's boiling over.'

Inevitably, Maggie's mother disapproved of the new just-above-the-knee printed skirt with the built-in petti-coat, not to mention Maggie's enthusiasm for all things Dutch and 'contemporary'. At school, she gained kudos from mentioning Henk this and Henk that at every opportunity.

During the summer, the school Heads condescended to allow a Sixth Form Society as a sop to the need for interaction between the sexes. There were Beetle Drives, debates and quizzes and lots of orange squash. At the end of each term there was a Hop, where someone played records and everybody jigged about or watched nonchalantly.

By the end of the Lower 6th, Maggie had her eye on a boy called Laurence. She'd sidle up to him, try to engage him in conversation, looked out for him around town on Saturday mornings, but he wasn't exactly encouraging.

'What you need is a new frock for the Hop, and a new hair style, then he'll take notice of you,' said Pauline, who was going steadyish with a boy called Rob who'd moved in next door to her.

The Dutch girls came over before the end of term, bringing swathes of fashionable fabric. They stitched and whirred on Maggie's grandmother's sewing machine and oohed and aahed at the finished product as Maggie twirled around in the full gathered skirt. Maggie's mother decreed it wouldn't be decent unless she wore a slip underneath the integral paper nylon underskirt.

It was the girls' school turn to host the Hop. Under the watchful eye of the caretaker, some of the boys had decked out the gym with festive lights and balloons in honour of the school leavers. Rob escorted the four friends into the hall. Maggie knew she looked good in the new frock; her hair gleamed; she'd at last mastered the art of mascara. Scanning around for Laurence, she saw him surrounded by his mates. Her eyes sparkled when he strode over to Rob's harem. Perhaps he'd prefer to dance with

Anneke, or Kaatje… but no, he chose her. What bliss! Someone had smuggled in some cider. Laurence offered her a glass, nectar to her unaccustomed taste buds as she gulped it down.

Then there was a tap on her shoulder, a Dutch whisper in her ear.

'De melk gekookt boven!'

Love Divine, All Loves Excelling

Sophie Loveday stood on tiptoe to see herself in the mirror. She adjusted her ruff, combed the parting in her sleek pale hair, noticed how well her eyes reflected the Virgin Mary blue of her cassock. Yes. Adam would notice her alright. He'd probably congratulate her on her solo verse in 'Once in Royal David's City' not to mention 'Jesus Christ the Apple Tree'. Bound to. Never mind that this was her third rendition — what a pompous word, much loved by her father. *Grr!* Fathers were *so* annoying, particularly when they were Vicars and supposed to be perfect.

Disregarding the tittle-tattle, the odd last minute hum of tricky bars, she peeked out through the choir vestry door. Despite the chill, the church was abuzz with anticipation, hardly a spare seat in sight. Of course St Edmund's Carol Service wouldn't be as good as King's, but the choir was pretty good — even Sophie's GCSE music teacher said her years as head chorister would look good on her CV. Such a pity Organ Morgan was so laid back as to be practically horizontal. He'd never improve Choir standards in a year of Sundays, however much he over-indulged his power complex by playing interminable, virtuoso voluntaries. Still, the one soaring out from the back of the church was pretty cool.

'Right folks, time to line up,' stage-whispered her father and gathered the clergy and choir into a procession in front of The Tombs. This space, tucked in beside the sanctuary, had a wonderful acoustic. Her father stepped up to the lectern to welcome the twice-a-year congregation.

Adam Godley, the curate, had been at King's— he'd met his wife Sonia there. Whenever she babysat for Adam, Sophie suffered a frisson of jealousy whenever she saw the big smiling photo over the chimney breast. Adam was punting, Sonia laughing up into his face. Poor Adam, to lose his wife like that, so young, and those poor motherless children. Her father said Adam had begged for a second curacy in Little Baddenham, so his parents could help out with the toddlers. Sophie, like Juliet, had fallen irrevocably in love with him at first sight. Adam invaded her every thought. She'd even gone to his confirmation classes, having spurned her father's instruction.

She'd never told her love, not even to Penny, the closed to a best friend she had. When the other girls at school wittered on about how far they'd gone with this, that and the other boy, Sophie remained aloof, particularly when Penny told her to take that silly Mona Lisa smile off her face.

Candles sputtered into life; the nave lights dimmed; a brief silence; then the organ launched into her intro. Sophie breathed extra deeply to settle her nerves, then, as yet invisible to the congregation, her voice drifted pure and sweet into the high-arched roof. As the choir joined in for the second verse, the procession set off decorously down the central aisle, then the congregation shambled to its feet. Sophie glanced back and caught Adam's eye: he smiled, gave her a thumbs up. *O joy!* 'For He is our childhood's pattern...' From the choir stalls at the back of the church, Sophie was able to gaze her fill. Lessons were read, carols were sung, a bunch of primary school children gathered to sing 'Away in a Manger' under the direction of their teacher.

Sophie took her time putting away her music and robes, then tidying up after everybody else, thus contriving to be one of the last to leave. Adam and her father were bidding farewell to the last members of the congregation. They must be frozen in the icy blast from the church porch. Sophie knew for a fact that her father wore thermals under his cassock. *Gross!* She couldn't picture Adam in thermals... She lurked behind a pillar. Adam was deep in conversation with the primary school teacher, Miss Stuart. Sophie craned her ears.

'The children were magnificent, Vicky.' Was Adam touching her arm? He had a habit of touching parishioners' arms. 'They're lucky to have such an excellent trainer. Are you still OK for them to sing at the Christingle Service?'

'Yes, of course, we'll be there,' Miss Stuart was saying, 'and I'll make sure their parents come with the tinies. The children look so angelic carrying those oranges with the candles.'

'Bless you, Vicky, you're a star,' Adam was saying, grasping her hand as she left. He was famous for the fervour of his hand shake.

Sophie emerged from her pillar just as Adam was clanging the door shut.

'Sophie,' he beamed, pressing her hand in his. 'Your solo was magnificent, you're a star!'

'Thank you,' she smiled into his eyes. 'It was better my first time.'

'Nonsense! It couldn't have been better, not even at King's.'

But he hadn't been there three years ago, he'd been burying his wife in his old parish. Sophie nearly fainted with joy.

'Are you by any chance free on New Year's Eve?'

Oh Joy! Was he asking her out? 'Would you be OK to babysit?' he was saying. 'I don't like asking you, but something's come up, and my parents will be sunning themselves in Majorca. I expect you youngsters have got better things to do, but I'd be very grateful…'

'No problem, you know you can always count on me.'

'If you're quite sure, Sophie…'

What friends? She hadn't really wanted to go to the Youth Centre. That time of night, with all the rowdies out, Adam would have to walk her home, even ask her to stay the night...

'I'll be there.' She floated on cloud nine all the way home, texting Penny to cancel their New Year plans.

She'd make her usual cake for Adam. Unlike Sophie's mum, Adam's mother never baked for coffee mornings. According to Sophie's mum, Mrs Godley and her husband had been none too pleased when Adam had taken the curacy in Little Baddenham—they felt Adam was taking advantage of them. Adam's mother seemed to like her, though Sophie found her a tad intimidating.

Sophie loved baby-sitting: the bedtime stories; the independence of having total control over Adam's TV; the privilege of having the run of the place. Sometimes she lay down on Adam's big double bed. Perhaps it would be their baby one day... If parishioners called while Adam was helping her with her RE project, she positively glowed when she made tea for them.

Meanwhile, there was Midnight Mass, Christmas dinner and the paraphernalia of presents. On Boxing Day, she'd settle down to completing her coursework and revision, just in case there were developments with Adam... She'd allow herself some time off, and make gingerbread men for the children... Of course, if she married Adam, there would be no point in going to Uni. At the Fair Trade coffee morning, Adam's mother had mentioned that lemon drizzle was his favourite.

*****

When Sophie looked out of the window first thing on New Year's Eve, the garden was white with a fine powdering of snow. Perhaps she'd have to stay the night at Adam's if Little Baddenham got snowed in.

'Better late than never,' said Sophie's mother,' who got stupidly sentimental about white Christmases. *Gross!* She'd finished the coursework, reached her revision target, done the baking. Sophie idled the afternoon away, unable to settle to anything. Perhaps the babysitting was just a ruse to get her to the Curate's House, and they'd stay in together, sipping wine over a roaring fire… She found herself reciting Juliet's soliloquy: 'Gallop apace, you fiery-footed steeds And bring in cloudy night immediately…'

The landline rang. 'It's Adam for you dear,' called Sophie's mum, 'about the babysitting.'

Was he going to cancel? But no.

'You'd best bring an overnight bag Sophie, just in case. You never know when the weather's like this. Would that be OK?'

'Yes, of course,' breathed Sophie.

'Best hand me back to your mother so she knows everything's in order.'

Wow! Lucky Auntie Sue had given her a proper grownup dressing gown and nightie, sexy or what.

'To tell you the truth Adam, I'm glad she's babysitting for you rather than gallivanting with the rowdy youth,' her mum was saying.

*****

Shivering, Sophie rang Adam's doorbell, cake-tin in her gloved hand. He was already in his overcoat, looking very smart. *Did he have his dog collar on under that scarf?*

'I'm *so* grateful,' he said, squeezing her hand. 'Help yourself to whatever you like, there's J²0 in the fridge. Ella's out for the count, but I expect Matt would like a story. Bye then,' and he rushed past her into the snowy street.

Matt didn't drop off till she'd read most of the fairy stories in his book twice. She went downstairs, contemplated a glass of wine, poured some juice, helped herself to nibbles and went through to the lounge. Adam had laid the fire, but not lit it, though the Christmas tree and decorations were twinkling cheerfully. Sophie yearned to try the cake, but it would be rude to cut it if he wasn't there, after all it was a present. Before turning on the TV, she pulled the curtains aside and looked out at the Christmas-card scene. *Come night, come Romeo.* Funny, Adam's car was still there. The more she looked, the more it was still parked there. Someone must have given him a lift...

She stretched out on the sofa, snuggled into a cosy throw, watched the celebrations, heard the midnight chimes, gasped at the fireworks, dozed off with Juliet's words skittering in and out of her brain.

Much later, she woke. Adam hadn't said where he'd been going. Perhaps he was snowed up. A glance through the window showed only an inch or two of snow Perhaps he'd had an accident...

She'd get a drink, her taste buds craved hot chocolate. What if there was only Ovaltine? She hated Ovaltine. Funny, there was a narrow strip of light coming under the kitchen door. Surely she had switched it off? Mum had always been fussy about not wasting electricity and saving the planet.

She opened the door, took one step and stood stock still. That Miss Stuart was sitting at the kitchen table as if she owned the place. There was a fizzing bottle and two glasses beside her. Sophie could hear Adam's feet coming down the stairs, then his voice.

'The kids are OK darling.'

He was close behind her in the doorway, almost breathing down her neck. A little nervous cough. 'Oh it's you Sophie.'

Who else could it be?

'You were fast asleep, so we decided not to wake you,' said Miss Stuart.

'Come and join us,' said Adam.

That Miss Stuart was reaching up into the cupboard for a third glass, her ring finger dazzling.

WHERE THERE'S HOPE

Marcus Phillips had been born middle aged, for he shunned all things trendy and refused point blank to smoke or do drugs or go clubbing. As for girls, Jack, his nearest approximation to a friend, summed it up by saying, 'He wouldn't know what to do with a girl if he had one.' For Marcus was a loner, devoted to study and solitary pursuits, exceedingly gauche and the apple of his mother's eye. Kate, his precocious little sister, at fourteen, had already dated half the Lower Sixth at Little Baddenham High School.

It wasn't till after Christmas that it dawned on Marcus that Sophie Loveday, the Vicar's daughter, seemed to want him to notice her. He often caught her gazing at him soulfully across the refectory and she would linger at his table in the library asking to look at his notes.

'She fancies you,' said Jack. 'Why don't you ask her out?' Marcus blushed furiously and mumbled about work. But as the long evenings drew out, his studies suffered because he couldn't get Sophie out of his head. The vision of golden hair framing her delicate face and her wide enigmatic smile haunted him, but the thought of actually approaching her provoked instant paralysis. He would rehearse his little speech: 'Sophie, I don't suppose you'd like to come out with me? I could get some tickets for *The Return of the King.*' But the time was never right. Besides, permanent suspense would be preferable to the axe blow to his dreams and the humiliation he would suffer if rejected.

He had high hopes of the Geography Field Trip to the Peak District in March. Surely he would find an appropriate moment to ask her.

*****

He'd bungled his self-conscious attempt to sit beside her on the mini-bus, he'd failed to get close to her in Castleton Youth Hostel, but after a couple of days, there they were, striding along the ridge together, a little apart from the main group, with Back Tor looming ahead, and beyond, the softer contours of Lose Hill. The wind buffeted them relentlessly and whipped up the scudding clouds, whose shadows swept along the distant landscape to the north in an ever changing pattern of fantastic shapes.

'Look Marcus, it's like an enormous bird flapping down the hillside.'

'Like the eagles that air-lifted the hobbits. And now it's a dragon, with a spiky back and breathing fire.'

'It must be Smaug.'

They laughed contentedly — wonder of wonders, a shared devotion to Tolkien. Here was his opening. *Sophie, I don't suppose...* But his words would be swept away by the wind and he'd feel foolish shouting. Marcus yearned to put his arm round Sophie to protect her from the monster, but the moment and the dragon had passed.

Hope Valley shimmered in pale water-colour tints below the gently falling southern slope of the hill.

'Even the Cement Works have an ethereal quality, Marcus.'

'It's like a fairy-tale castle from up here.'

'Or the Two Towers.'

'Come on Sophie, we must catch up with the others. Marcus was so happy to be alone with Sophie — but he didn't want to spoil this wonderful day by causing comment.

'Not to worry.' They route-marched on. Back Tor loomed ever more dramatically as they approached.

'Do you mind if I do a quick sketch Marcus?' Sophie rummaged around in her back-pack for drawing materials. 'Could you fill out my worksheet?' Marcus found a little hollow, just big enough for two to sit well out of the blustering wind, and spread out his waterproof for her.

'It's almost snug here.' He got out the worksheets and packed lunches while she drew Back Tor, towering bleakly above with a sparse row of conifers straggling lopsidedly down the gentle slope towards Hope.

'It's carboniferous limestone underneath all this lot,' pronounced Marcus. 'Glacial action, millions of years ago, shaped the valleys, and water and wind erosion have done the rest. The limestone's actually soluble you know.'

Sophie pointed her pencil at the loose scree that covered the hillside further down. 'I suppose that's the example of wind erosion? And what about all those little hummocks further down?'

'You mean the drumlins? They're built up from the residue of the glacier.'

Sophie put in the finishing touches to her sketch, a few spare, bold lines.

'It's wonderful Sophie. You're a genius.'

'Here, I'd like you to have it.'

'But I couldn't possibly. It's too much part of yourself to give away.' But she would take no refusal.

'I'll treasure it always. Tell you what, I'll photocopy it for you. I could even blow it up.'

'You're my hero.' Sophie was packing up frenziedly. 'I'll eat on the hoof.'

Greatly daring, Marcus got to his feet and held out his hand to help her up, but what with the backpacks, and the sandwiches, their hands made no further contact. He'd never be able to ask her out if he couldn't even hold her hand.

They hurried on, and eventually came upon the others, sprawled out on a sheltered plateau, admiring the view of Hope Brink just beyond the trig point on Lose Hill.

'Come along, what've you two been up to?' grinned Jack.

'Having a quick snog I expect,' smirked Tom.

Marcus was enveloped by a hot and cold blush.

'We won't make Win Hill at this rate,' said Smithy, 'or the coffee shop at Castleton.'

They set off in pairs, but Marcus was too timid to help Sophie over the next, or any subsequent, stile. Someone might see. But perhaps in the Caves tomorrow... He pictured himself protecting the fair maiden from the terrors of the unknown, guiding her stumbling feet along the rough-hewn steps, the slippery slopes. Hand in hand, they would gaze in awe at the weird formations. Perhaps, in the half darkness of the Mines of Moria, he would no longer feel inhibited.

*****

Treak Cliff Cavern more than lived up to Marcus's expectations, until disaster struck. Taking Sophie's hand was the most natural thing in the world as they followed the guide along the well-lit, smooth tracks and steep steps that led to the subterranean world of the Blue John Mine. The subtly illuminated colours of the rocks were a revelation. Did Sophie also feel an overwhelming erotic arousal at the sight of the rigid stalactites bearing down upon the up rearing stalagmites in this magnificent womb of the earth? Her hand responded to his squeeze as they pointed out to each other the intriguing formations that emerged from the amber flowstone. The translucent shapes looked as soft as beeswax, for all they'd taken millions of years to grow. Marcus and Sophie were almost oblivious of the small children who had been doing their best to ruin the fantasy world with unseemly shrieks and comments.
  'Looks like pink wibbly wobbly worms.'
  'No. It's bunches of carrots.'
  'Looks more like a load of little willies to me.'

'D'you think Gollum's down there? Precioussss. Sssss.'

Sophie's body willingly met his as he put his arm round her in the half light of the golden, glowing Dreamland. Dare he kiss her? 'Sophie,' he began, 'I don't suppose you'd like to...' but the guide burst in:

'It's customary at this point to let you experience total darkness.'

The lights went out. The black velvet silence was uncanny. Marcus never knew which of them made the first move, but their lips met tentatively, then explored delightedly. But the darkness bored into him, the weight of millions of tons of rock, the myriad writhing formations crowded in on him. His mouth left Sophie's, he was shaking all over in a cold sweat. She caught him as he stumbled and landed on the hard floor of the cave. When the lights blazed on, Sophie was bending over him like the Lady Galadriel, forcing his head between his knees, calmly reassuring him, offering him a sip of water.

'It's all right Marcus, just take it easy.' The guide bustled up, followed by Mr Smith, who attempted to keep the others back.

'Feeling a bit woozy? It takes some people like that,' said the guide.

'But I feel such a fool.' His breath was coming in great gasps, and he hadn't even brought his inhaler.

'Don't worry Marcus. It doesn't matter, honestly.' And he clung to Sophie childishly as she helped him along the passage to the outside world.

While they were in the mine, it had clouded over, and the bright sunshine had gone out of the day.

*****

Barricaded in by his rucksack, Marcus sat brooding in splendid isolation as the minibus sped through the flashing lights of the night. Why did the best things always go wrong for him? He'd really been getting somewhere with Sophie. He'd held her hand, kissed her, but the words remained unsaid. What must she think of him after his ignominious collapse? He'd never be able to speak to her again, ever.

When they stopped for a comfort break at Cambridge Services, Marcus stayed alone in the minibus. By the time the rest piled noisily back, he was half asleep and decided to remain so. Then he felt someone taking the place of his rucksack. That someone leant into him comfortingly. Cautiously, he opened his eyes to find Sophie clutching an envelope.

'Marcus, I don't suppose you'd like to go and see *The Return of the King?* Jack's taking your sister and he's got a couple of spare tickets.' Sophie smiled into his eyes and took his hand in hers.

'Cool,' he murmured.

THE CRUICKSHANK CHRONICLES II
ALL THAT GLISTERS IS NOT GOLD

Whenever Anthony Cruickshank, or Tony as he now preferred to be called, took his family to visit his mother Laura, she insisted, weather permitting, that they all sit out in the orchard. However hard he tried to push it to the back of his mind, Tony was continually haunted by the picture of himself and his brother, Julian, digging their father's grave. Six feet deep they'd dug, far into the night, sweat dripping, clouds scudding across the moonlit sky.

Ironically, when Tony had met blond, beautiful Barbara at Great Baddenham Amateur Dramatic Society's rehearsals, he'd been playing both the Ghost of Hamlet's Father and First Gravedigger. Barbara had been roped in as Costume Mistress for the production. It had been love at first sight. Tony was initially reluctant to let his wife into the close-guarded family secret. Not that it was illegal, his barrister brother had made certain of that and Avril, his wife, had inside knowledge of the Health and

Safety rulings which had been observed scrupulously, but it wouldn't do for Barbara to blurt it out to all and sundry. For, as his mother had pointed out when he first brought her home, Barbara was, undeniably, outspoken. Instead of admiring Tony's late father's ubiquitous antiques, Barbara had condemned Laura's treasures as 'out-of-date-trash.'

'You'd better watch it dear,' Laura said behind her hand as Barbara left the drawing room, 'she's not going to be content with calling a spade a spade, she might embarrass you with "bloody shovels."'

'But Mother,' Tony bridled in defence of his love, 'that's because she's scrupulously honest, as well as a perfectionist.'

'She's beautiful, she's besotted with you,' Laura said, 'if you love her, you'd better snap her up before someone else does. She'll be an excellent home-maker, in spite of her Estuary English.'

*****

The young couple frequently brought the three children to visit their grandmother. They romped happily in the extensive grounds under the supervision of their Auntie Rosie if she happened to be around. Rosie was a stalwart pusher of the swing that hung from the pear tree, an expert at hiding and seeking and dusting down the children's smart clothes to forestall their mother's nagging.

They were all sitting in the orchard beside the pear tree one Saturday, basking in the sun, sipping home-made lemonade and watching the children play.

There had been an awkward moment when Timmy had asked to borrow a spade.

'I want to dig a hole to Australia, Grandma,' he insisted. Tony's pulse started racing, but Laura got in before Barbara had a chance to come out with something embarrassing — Avril had let slip the taboo subject of the burial site years ago, but they were all agreed that the next generation should remain in ignorance.

'Not in the flower bed, darling, why don't you try near the pond, the soil will be softer there.'

'Why?'

The girls clamoured for spades too and they set to work happily, joined by Laura's cat, Tiddles, who was on the lookout for wiggling worms to toy with.

'Isn't this nice dears?' said Laura with her sweetest smile. 'Such a pity you can't be with the children every day, Barbara.' Tony, seething, opened his mouth to protest, but Barbara got in before him.

'I'd be bored stiff stuck in the house all day, and I'm only part-time, it's not as if I bring much work home with me seeing as I teach needlework. Being a mere housewife would be a wicked waste of my education. Besides, we need the money to pay the mortgage.' They'd recently moved to a brand new, bigger house in Ipswich.

'It's not like when you were young, Mother.' Tony failed to keep the anger out of his voice. 'Most women have to juggle work and childcare these days. The kids are perfectly happy at nursery school, it's not as if they go every day. You were lucky enough to have private means, an ancestral home, a husband with an army pension and a talent for making money more or less honestly from antiques. Our generation have never had it that good.'

'Talk about privilege,' snorted Barbara, 'your class don't know the first thing about real life.'

Silence fell.

All three avoided eye contact.

Laura took a deep breath.

'But it's so bad for the little ones to be deprived of mother-love. I could help you out financially, you know, at least until they're all at school.'

'No way,' chorused the couple, throwing each other outraged glances.

Tony, however, had a sneaking feeling that his mother had a point.

At lunch in the farm-house kitchen, Barbara was particularly authoritative on the matter of no-pudding-unless-you-have-an-empty-plate, and kicked Laura's cat when he was discovered under the table snaffling up offerings dropped accidentally-on-purpose.

Barbara's home was always immaculate with never a toy out of place, never a trace of paint when the kids had been daubing pictures. There was always a cup of coffee or a meal for friends who were invited, or just dropped in, to take solace from their camaraderie and perfect home. Tony was a lucky man, he knew it, to have such a happy marriage, so beautiful a wife and his three lovely children.

By the time the youngest was out of nappies, Tony, though he loved his wife dearly, grew vaguely aware of something missing. As a boy at Little Baddenham College, and later at university, he'd been a leading light in the dramatic society. He'd also enjoyed landscape painting and photography. Barbara had no empathy with these pursuits. If they visited a beauty spot, Tony yearned to linger and glory in the scene before him and to fix it on film if not on paper. But, after dispensing orange juice, Barbara would be hustling him on with a casual 'very pretty.'

'For heaven's sake, Barbara, what's the hurry?'

Now Tony was a people-person and took to bringing home lame ducks to sort them out: youngsters from the office who couldn't cope; blokes from the camera club with failing marriages.

'How can they expect me to do their tax-returns when all they give me is a shoe-box full of illegible receipts? And it's always at the last minute Tone…' Jim, or Charlie, or Wayne would complain.

'My wife doesn't understand me,' Ed would moan. 'She whinges on about my extravagance. She has plenty of house-keeping money, and I never begrudge her a new dress, but if I want to buy the latest lens, it's always, "but we can't afford such luxuries, dear, you take such lovely shots with the one you have." She makes my life hell, Tone.'

Barbara would feed them before turning in for an early night, leaving the men to put the world to rights. In the morning, she'd shush the children to protect the sleeper, swathed like a mummy in a sleeping bag, on the sofa.

Tony's little sister Rosie and her disastrous love life was a frequent visitor.

He thrived on the stimulation and the sense of good doing. Barbara didn't complain, but her silence suggested resignation rather than sympathy. Tony was on tenterhooks waiting for the bloody-shovel moment when Barbara would come out with a comment about wasters and no-hopers.

One evening, Tony brought home a maiden in distress from the camera club. Sylvia was failing dismally at her teaching practice, perhaps Barbara could help.

'Poor girl! She had some sort of break down. They should never have signed her off so soon. She's cooped up in a ghastly bedsit working all hours, it does her good to get out.'

Sylvia was thin, almost emaciated, with a wan complexion, thin mousy hair straggling limply to her shoulders. Her eyes were piercingly light blue, almost silver. She adored the children and became their favourite baby-sitter and Tony took her woes in hand. She became such a regular occupant of the sofa that Tony suggested she move in.

'It would only be till the end of the school term, Barbara.'

'I suppose we could squeeze the kids in together so she can have a room. Bloody anorexic won't take up much space.'

Tony kissed her. 'You're a star. Having a live-in babysitter will be so good—we can get out to the theatre and cinema more, you'd like that, wouldn't you.'

Barbara didn't respond.

When Laura came to call, she took Tony aside. 'That girl's clearly infatuated with you. Her eyes follow you round like a besotted puppy. Watch it Anthony, I don't want my grand-children growing up in a broken home.'

'There's nothing like that Mother, I'm just giving her a spot of counselling.'

Tony, however, had a sneaking feeling that his mother had a point.

Henceforth, he'd keep his distance and avoid sitting on the sofa during the midnight sessions.

One bright Saturday they all got up in the small hours to listen to the dawn chorus in Christchurch Park. Barbara busied herself identifying the bird calls for the children, while Tony and Sylvia listened, enraptured, to the music.

Another weekend, they took the campervan to Dunwich Heath, bundled up snuggly to watch the sunrise from the cliff top. Even Barbara was moved, particularly by the plaintiff shrieks of seabirds, but when the kids discovered the tide was out far enough for a thin band of sand, they dragged their mother down the path to the shore to make sand castles.

Tony stayed in the van to brew up for a second breakfast while Sylvia wandered off to gaze out to sea. The sun was up by now but there were still streaks of liquid pink and orange. Tony longed to paint it, but found his art materials had mysteriously disappeared from the van.

Poor Sylvia, she looked so solitary, so vulnerable on the skyline. He padded up to her with his Nikon round his neck. A tear or two was creeping down her face. He put an avuncular arm around her, and the moment stood still: an electric current of connection nearly knocked him over as she snuggled into him. The beauty of the seascape was charged with an intensity Tony hadn't felt since his student days. So this was what romantic love was about. Aware of his responsibilities, he drew apart awkwardly, muttering about making hot drinks.

Back at home, he did his best to avoid being alone with Sylvia. It wouldn't do for Barbara to guess, not that he was going to leave Barbara, their marriage was rock solid and he didn't want to hurt the children.

Of course Barbara did notice, she could hardly miss the adoring eyes.

'I think Sylvia had better leave,' she said, 'before things get out of hand. I trust you absolutely Tone, but it's not fair on her.'

However, moving her on proved a problem. Sylvia didn't get on with her family and she had nowhere to go till the end of the holidays.

One evening, just before term started, Barbara had an unavoidable PTA meeting. Sylvia shut herself in her room with a book, but when Tony came upstairs to check on the children, she was lurking on the landing, wraith-like in her dressing gown. The clinch was inevitable, the long kiss as charged as the embrace on the cliff top.

In bed that night, Tony confessed the kiss to Barbara, who remained stoical.

Sylvia did move on — back to college briefly but then to the mental hospital.

*****

Tony's sister, Rosie, had appeared slightly miffed when Sylvia had displaced her as principal sofa-guest, but they had a lot in common and had soon became friends. Next time Rosie turned up to bewail her troubles, she asked after Sylvia.

'She's back in the loony-bin,' said Barbara with pursed lips, 'and I hope she bloody well stays there.' She swanned off to yet another vital meeting. Alone with Rosie, Tony confided in her.

'She was desperately in love with me Sis, even Mother noticed. It was hard to resist, but it didn't get as far as an affair — Barbara knows all about it you may be sure, but no-one else. Just one cuddle, gazing out to sea, one kiss, one fumbled kiss, that sort of thing.'

'Poor you — it's usually me poring out my troubles into your ears. I find the role reversal flattering.'

'It's so good to be able to talk about it, Sis. It's over, and I'll never see her again. There's no question of leaving Barbara and splitting up the family. But those few romantic encounters brought home to me what's lacking in our marriage. Barbara's too down to earth to appreciate culture. I'll never have that glow of sense experience again, never be so moved by the beauty of nature or art.'

For once in his life, Tony had stripped his soul to his kid sister, but it came hard, for he knew Rosie had him on a pedestal. She looked thoughtful.

'Yes you can. I can see your Miranda has an artistic streak — you can share the aesthetic with your daughter when she's older.'

He smiled. 'I suppose… Thanks Rosie. Could you do me a favour?'

'Depends what it is.'

'You get on well with Sylvia, don't you?'

'Of course.'

'Could you manage to keep in touch with her? I need to know she's got over the puppy-love….

'You mean you want to assuage your guilty conscience? I'll try. On one condition. You must tell Ma that the non-affair of the year is over, finished, caput. She's been nearly out of her mind with worry.'

A Long Wait.

'Look into my eyes,' says the Aussie-voiced optician with wiggly blond hair. Last time, I'd seen the curly-haired hunk with deep-set brown eyes.

'I'll just chick that you're looking through the right part of your linses.' She fiddles around, kidnaps my glasses and disappears head-last to the basement limbo.

I can't hear straight without my specs. When I'd been carted off to the labour ward without them, I was so disorientated that my pre-natal advice evaporated.

Now, there is no demarcation, nothing to do except glance around muzzily: disembodied heads ascending and descending, but no wiggly blondes.

Idly, I pick up the Near Sight Check Chart, hold it two inches from my nose: *this is the smallest print in normal use*. It dawns on me that the numbers beside the words correspond with the point sizes on computer fonts. It's good to learn something new...

How much longer?

Those also serve who only sit and wait...

Still no Wiggly Hair.

The street door opens, a draught: a faceless female, draped in flowing ethnic cotton, approaches the counter and addresses Deep-set-Brown-Eyes.

'I'm not a regular customer, but I wonder if you can help me? The alignment on my varifocals is out of sync.'

The autocratic intonation rings a bell.

When?

Where?

It's rude to stare.

Have they kidnapped her glasses too? Can she see me? I can just make out lens-cleaning movements. Deep-set-Brown-Eyes holds the specs up, flexes their arms.

'I'm sure we can adjust the position.'

'I'm a musician,' she says, 'I'm performing in a concert in Cambridge tonight. I need to see both the music, and the conductor. At the same time. You do understand?'

The years peel back to the Cecilia's Singers days and the worst betrayal of my life. I can picture her sweetest smile…

But it can't be Jaqui, not in Ipswich… The voice continues. It must be Jaqui. She exudes elegance. If only I could penetrate the thick layers of purblindness…

I hold the check-board mirror-side up. I peer at my greying hair, the crow's feet. She, still skinny, probably wouldn't recognise me…

I can't catch her eye. *'Excuse me, is it Jaqui?'* would seem foolish if it wasn't her. Do I really want to break the silence of half a lifetime? There is no protocol for this situation.

At last, Wiggly Hair looms up with my glasses.

'If you can just look straight ahid.' I do. Out of the corner of my eye, the Indian cotton swims into focus, but, masked by the blond ringlets, the figure remains faceless.

The optometrist seizes my glasses, fiddles around. Blind again. Jaqui, if it be she, is getting up and graciously thanking Deep-set Brown Eyes. It must be her. My sight restored, I see the back of her highlighted hair receding.

Will she turn round?

Should I shout out, rush after her? But no, I am invisibly chained.

I've been waiting thirty years for the opportunity to ask her why she nicked my husband.

This story could have been a postscript for my novel,
Too Many Tenors

Over the Top

'Stop, stop the car. Now. I mean it.'

Barry, set and sullen faced, swerved to the side of the road with a screech of brakes that all but overrode his wife's hysterical outburst.

'Give me the keys. I'm driving, you can fucking well get home on your own flat feet. That is if you can ever find the way.'

Barry's mouth flapped up and down like a gold fish as he tried to find the words to brave the familiar onslaught.

'But we agreed, you'd drink and I'd drive. You're in no fit state to be behind that wheel, Belinda.'

'The only driving you're doing tonight is driving me round the bend. I said "right" not left you addlepated nerd, so why the hell did you turn left?' she fumed.

Barry really didn't know.

*****

The light-hearted banter had seemed quite funny at the office Christmas bash.

'Barry's mum used to read him *The 101 Dalmations* at bedtime.'

'And I always sympathized with poor old Missis who never could tell the difference between her right paw and her left paw, even when the spots were different!' This comment had brought about little ripples of laughter.

'D'you know what my idea of hell is?' Barry continued. 'It's going round and round a roundabout for all eternity because I don't know where to get off.' Trevor, his immediate boss, hooted and began refilling Barry's glass, but Belinda put her foot down and absolutely insisted on raiding the kitchen for pure apple juice.

Barry had a fleeting vision of the grief he'd invariably suffered at 1st Little Baddenham Scouts be-cause of his inability to grasp the vagaries of the OS maps used on hikes. None of the others had seemed to understand his theory about how much easier it would be if everyone was just beamed up and down between locations like in *Star Trek*.

*****

'The Keys, Barry, now!' Belinda was holding out her hand, the bracelet he'd given her for Christmas dangling seductively from her wrist.

'But...'

'No buts—I only had two glasses—you needn't worry your thick head about that.'

Barry undid his seat belt with great deliberation, withdrew the keys, got out, slammed the door, playing for time. Belinda shuffled over into the driver seat, pulling her pashmina tight around her shoulders.

'Keys Barry.' She opened the window, letting in a bitter blast of all too fresh air, then leant over and snicked down the passenger door lock.

'Come off it Belinda, even you can't expect me to walk home in this weather. Besides, I haven't a clue where we are.'

'You've made that abundantly obvious.'

Stony silence.

'Really Belinda, your behaviour is outrageous, totally OTT. At least let me get my coat.'

'Oh, get back in then if you must, but this is the very last time I ever sit beside you in this car. I mean it. And that'll really cramp your style. I can't understand how you ever get anywhere when you're on your own.'

Barry couldn't either.

'You've no idea what it's like to be born without a bump of direction,' he pleaded. 'I reckon it's a missing gene.' Belinda laughed, in spite of herself.

*****

'What is it?' said Barry, tearing off the birthday paper.

'A Sat-Nav. Satellite Navigation. That should sort you out once and for all.'

'Oh Belinda, you shouldn't have, it's much too expensive.'

'Not if it saves our marriage.'

Barry wasn't at all convinced that the marriage was saveable, or even worth saving. It wasn't as if they had kids.

Now Barry was a whiz at computers. He sat fiddling with the Sat-Nav for the rest of the day, and set it up for the trip to Hintlesham Hall, their birthday treat restaurant. He insisted on driving. Never a cross word, never a miss-crossed road.

'In two hundred yards, go straight on over the roundabout, take the second exit… In fifty yards, turn right.' He hadn't been in the habit of measuring distances in 100 yard units, but after a few too early turns into cul-de-sacs—'turn round wherever possible'—he soon got the hang of it.

His life was transformed. He felt liberated, a hitherto unexperienced confidence filled his every fibre, and it was all down to Jane, the Sat-Nav lady or Lady Janetta as he re-named his mentor.

'Stop fiddling with that thing! You've driven to your mother's every fortnight for the last fifteen years. Even you can't get lost between here and Little Baddenham!' Belinda taunted.

But Barry delighted in the sound of Lady Janetta's exquisitely clear voice, her lucid instructions, her endless patience, even the little undertone of criticism when she had to repeat, 'You have reached your destination.' Sometimes she said it in the middle of the night when she was on charge. He found this positively stimulating, and he even felt moved to make love to his wife, fantasising the while.

'You know Belinda, it's almost as good as being beamed up—no more poring over the map, you just key in the address and blow me you're there.'

Increasingly, he had this feeling, that there was a bit missed out of his normal life between the here and the there, where only Lady Janetta was meaningful for him. What did she look like? Blond? Dark? He was sure she had blue eyes. He found himself looking out for her wherever he went. 'That's her,' he'd say to himself, as a figure slipped in and out of the corner of his eye. Lady Janetta was his saviour, the one who had metamorphosed him from near inadequacy into a confident self-sufficient being.

*****

Barry set Lady Janetta increasingly difficult tasks, involving long, intricate routes. Sometimes he made a deliberate mistake to test her out, but she never failed him. She took a second or two to calculate an alternative route, put him back on course and, if all else failed, commanded him to turn round wherever possible.

Meanwhile, Belinda, trust her, was getting quite uptight about the whole thing, and hummed and hah-ed and complained that he never let her drive, and moreover he was always out and they never had any quality time together. She seemed to have entirely forgotten her Christmas ultimatum.

*****

Eventually, it all came spilling out.

'You've got another woman. Go on, admit it, you've got another woman.'

Barry denied it, of course, but not at all convincingly, because in a way it was true, he had got another woman, the ephemeral Lady Janetta who, day by day, was becoming more and more real to him. Why, sometimes, she even forsook her script and addressed him personally.

'Now Barry, see what a fine man you've become, decisive, a first class driver, on the spot, why don't you put in for promotion?'

Belinda had been on at him for years to better himself, complaining that he didn't earn enough and marking up job adverts in the East Anglian, but after a few unadmitted applications, Barry had given up, convinced that he belonged near the bottom of the pile.

When Lady Janetta pointed out that Trevor was on the move, and his job would be available for the asking, Barry bearded the boss, got a huge pay rise and a posh company car, into which he instantly transferred Lady Janetta, the joy of his life. He didn't actually mention the promotion to his wife for fear of all those 'I told you so's.' Besides, his success was all the sweeter since it was a secret between him and his true love. He made a seemingly generous gift of his share in the old car.

'You might as well get it insured in your name Belinda, since you're the sole user.' Belinda was delighted, but still suspicious.

On the rare occasions when Belinda joined him in the new car, there hardly seemed room for the three of them.

'Why don't you get into the back, dear?' he'd suggest, but this enraged her even more, and she complained about that bitch's perfume polluting the atmosphere.

Little did she know!

Barry was seriously contemplating leaving boring Belinda, even giving her the house, and asking Lady Janetta to go away with him into the blue yonder.

Christmas came round once more, as it does, trailing beside it the office bash.

Barry dreamed of arriving with the delectable Lady Janetta on his arm, but of course it was Belinda that came with him, eyes on antennae to sniff out her rival. Naturally, he was driving, and she drinking, it was all agreed. The girls were in a huddle, getting loud and giggly, the chaps propping up the bar, chatting pie-eyed about work.

Out of the corner of his ear, Barry heard Kate from Reception gushing at Belinda.

'You must be so proud of him now he's Area Manager. Everyone's impressed with the change in him. I suppose it was down to that outward bound management course he went on.'

'What did you say?' There was a crashing silence as Belinda stalked across to Barry, her anger poised to spring.

'Why didn't you tell me you'd been promoted,' she shrieked.

Barry really didn't know. Desultory chat puttered into noisy talk.

*****

One day, Barry carelessly left the Sat-Nav at home — Belinda had been most insistent that he remove the unit every night for fear of thieves. Panic overwhelmed him as he drove, he was totally lost, eternally stuck on that hellish roundabout, hooted at and derided. He was two hours late for his appointment, and lost a contract for the firm. He tried to be blasé about the whole thing when Belinda enquired after his day.

Next morning, he was dimly aware that something about the settings on the Sat-Nav didn't seem right, but this factor flitted into insignificance in comparison with his transports of delight when he set out again with the delectable Lady Janetta beside him.

'Don't ever desert me again,' Barry pleaded.

'I thought it was more a case of your forgetting me.' Lady Janetta nuzzled up to him the way he liked, and kissed him tenderly on the cheek as he drove on. He drew up in a lay-by, and kissed her passionately.

'No way!'

'I'll be right with you till the end of the road,' Lady Janetta assured him after a long clinch.

'You mean you'll come away with me?'

'Why not? Where would you like to go today?'

Barry didn't care, anywhere would do as long as it was with her and without boring Belinda.

'A touch of sea air?'

'Sounds good.'

'Then off we go. At the next roundabout, turn left, first exit, then keep left...'

Before he realised it, they had beamed down somewhere near Eastbourne.

The road meandered up to Beachy Head, with the cloud-flecked sky above and the deep-blue sea below sparkling in the glittering sun, where larks warbled, and seagulls shrieked and butterflies fluttered above the flowers of the spring.

Tra la.

'Turn left, after fifty yards, bear left over the grass. At the end of the grass, drive straight on…'

This story was placed in the top five entries in the This Morning *Short Story Competition 2009*

The Eternal Quadrangle I
Love, Love Me Do

Lady Katherine Marriner sighed, toyed with her cucumber sandwiches in the elegant drawing room. Perhaps the expected sense of liberation would hit her once the fact of Archie's death had sunk in. Somehow, it palled into insignificance beside the news of the fatal shooting of President John F Kennedy.

In retrospect, their marriage had been so suitable: the Georgian manor house; the title; the security of an older man, but she had never really loved Captain Sir Archibald Marriner, DSO, RN. There had been a certain charm in the returning war hero, the bluff gallantry of an English squire and love and marriage had been all the thing in the roaring twenties. After all, she had not exactly been the belle of the ball. It might have worked out if only they'd had children... She put down her cup and saucer, dabbed at her lips with a napkin. Perhaps she should have married Bertie, the younger brother. They were more of an age and they would have been more intellectually compatible. Poor Bertie had been killed in 1939, leaving an infant son and a widow in straitened circumstances.

'Do you mind if Diana and the boy come and live here, old thing? Baddenham Hall is big enough in all conscience,' Archie had said. But the sisters-in-law had never really got on and Katherine had been relieved when Diana had remarried, albeit beneath her.

But now boring, predictable Archie was gone, there was an unaccountable emptiness. Instead of constantly slamming doors, thumping footsteps or irritating harrumphings over The Times at breakfast, there was silence. Perhaps, after the funeral, she would feel more like the liberated being she'd briefly become when she had her wild fling with Frank all those years ago. Poor old Archie, he'd never understood when she'd come clean about it, although he'd been having his own bits of fluff on the side for years.

Withdrawing her gaze from the lingering autumn leaves in the garden, Katherine decided she might as well get on with sorting out Archie's papers.

She went through to the library: a faint whiff of tobacco.

She switched on the wireless: racing commentary.

She tuned into the Light Programme: the Beatles' latest release — Archie had never countenanced popular music.

She sat down at his bureau and flicked absently through the drawers and cubby-holes: neat piles of yellowing bills; receipts from tailors, gunsmiths and book-makers; bulging files of letters relating to long-ago business transactions or charitable concerns. Most of them she dispatched to the wastepaper basket, the tattered remnants of an unremarkable life.

Then, tucked away in a supposedly 'secret' compartment, she found a fat bundle of letters tied up in faded red ribbon, her own love letters, she supposed. Odd, she did not remember writing so many. 'Love, love me do' relayed the wireless. She would never have put Archie down as a romantic hoarder, poor old thing. Katherine, fearing that sentiment might interrupt her thankless task, decided to postpone the pleasure of reading the letters till bedtime and her customary night cap. Besides, she did not really want the Higginses to catch her in a moment of weakness.

Then she came across a stiff legal envelope, his copy of the will no doubt. There would not be any surprises there. The estate was not actually entailed, but Archie had been a staunch believer in *primogeniture* and had decreed that everything would go to his nephew on his widow's demise. As she thought, the house and a comfortable income for her lifetime. But what was this? A codicil: a substantial sum 'to my daughter, Amanda Lovejoy, in recompense for the harm I did to her dear mother, Lucy.' Katherine blinked, gasped. A daughter? A daughter presupposed a mistress, but a 'dear mother?' And how dare Archie leave all that money to a perfect stranger. The codicil, she noted, had been witnessed by those Higginses.

Lucy? Wasn't there a portrait of some Lucy, an actress, was it, or a *diva* who'd lived there before

Admiral Sir James Marriner, enriched in the Napoleonic wars, had bought the Hall?

Katherine poured herself a stiff drink from Archie's not very secret stash, turned to the bundle of letters and ripped off the red ribbon. One glance revealed that the correspondence was indeed nothing to do with her. Perhaps her own letters lay buried deep within the confines of some old trunk in the attics. Perhaps not. After all, there had been few letters, and even less substance...

She put a match to the fire and settled into Archie's battered leather armchair, gulping at the whisky as she skimmed through the folded sheets, shedding an involuntary tear or two. Why, the liaison had continued for years, before and after her own tempestuous affair. The irony of it... The scandal of the King's association with Mrs Simpson raged in the late thirties: forbidden love was in the air. Perhaps that was what had spurred them on. 'Queen Wallis.' They'd all tried it out derisively.

Who would have thought the old man—although he had not been so old a quarter of a century ago—would have had so much love in him?

> *'Dearest Lucy, how I long to be with you. I am in a fever of suspense till we can meet again... I have never known such happiness as when I am in your presence...'*

Such drivel, but it was almost poetic in its intensity. Apparently Lucy had held out against his importunities for a long time, pleading impropriety and his responsibilities to his wife. Clever little trollop, to string him along.

*'My feelings for my wife are long since dead,
and hers for me; she does not understand me,
and seems increasingly remote, whereas you, my
dearest...'*

Eventually they had become rapturous lovers.

*'Darling Lucykins, I cannot bear to be absent
from you...I will leave my wife tomorrow if only
you will give the word. Come away with me...'*

*'Dearest Archie-Parchie, I love you utterly and
for ever, but you must not sacrifice your
position in society for me. Whoever heard of a
Master of Hounds living in sin, or worse,
divorced and what about the disgrace for your
poor wife?'*

Why, the self-same arguments her young lover had used when, despite his reserved occupation, he had volunteered in 1939. Poor Frank, to die so young, so unfulfilled. If only they had all been honest enough to acknowledge their feelings, she and Frank could have been together and perhaps Archie could have had his longed for male heir.

Refilling her glass, Katherine wondered where and when Archie and this Lucy had had their assignations, then remembered all those business trips to town, the over-concerned phone calls to enquire after her health. Katherine smiled, remembering the joyous hours of passion during his absence. She really could not find it in her heart to be seriously jealous of the mystery mistress, but what on earth had she found so attractive in Archie? Then the letters had changed.

'Dear Archie-Parchie, you must come at once. I find that I am 'in the family way.' Do not desert me now, I beg of you...'

But what was this? Archie protesting that, after all, he respected his wife, and could not desert her. His business interests were in a delicate state, and would not survive a scandal. In short, he could not risk being unable to support two establishments. He loved Lucy, and would give her financial assistance, or pay for an abortion if she so wished, but the affair must end. He wished to remain with his dear wife, who seemed to be frightfully overwrought and in need of support.

The correspondence abruptly ceased, with a savage scrawl from Lucy returning all his letters. If he was going to treat her like that, then she never wanted to see him again.

Yes, Katherine had needed him after Frank left her. She and Archie had actually got quite close for a while, busying themselves with village life, Digging for Victory, the evacuees. If only she'd known that he was capable of giving up the great love of his life for her sake, how different it might have been. Perhaps she would have been able to love him after all. But in those days, discussing their infidelities or even their own relationship frankly and openly had been unthinkable. She switched off the light, and lay back in her comfortable bed, a warm glow of love for her dead husband mitigating her disappointment that she would not be quite so wealthy a widow as she'd anticipated.

Then her thoughts turned to the girl, Archie's daughter, her stepdaughter. She supposed the family solicitor would be able to discover her whereabouts. And what of that Lucy? On the whole, Katherine thought she could meet them both with equanimity were the need to arise.

*****

The whole county turned out for the funeral. Charles, his uncle's heir, was there of course, with his twice widowed mother on one arm and a hitherto unknown young lady on the other. Pretty little thing... Charles was never short of girlfriends... As they came out of the church, a sudden burst of sunshine emphasized the stark lights and shades of the graveyard: a cold breeze swirled brilliant leaves around the gaping hole.

'We therefore commit his body to the ground,' the vicar was chanting, 'earth to earth, ashes to ashes, dust to dust...' Diana acknowledged her nod distantly. Why, that girl had a faint air of familiarity... The ancestors on the stairs perhaps... Then Charles was beside her.

'Aunt Katherine, may I introduce my fiancée, Amanda. Amanda Lovejoy.'

Katherine caught her breath, beamed euphorically, extended her hand, and then hugged the girl. All's well that ends well.

'Congratulations, my dears.'

'Love, Love me do, Love, Love me do', twirled round inside her head.

The Norfolk Canary, 1798

Miss. Lucy Lindoe simpered and curtsied deeply, as she had been taught, her blond ringlets jigging as she did so. The studied elegance belied her tattered gown. The audience applauded rapturously for they had not yet tired of the four-year-old's touching performance of 'I am little Bess the Ballad Singer'. She danced off into the wings.

'Was I not good, Papa' she lisped into his waiting arms.

'Excellent, child, but it is high time you learnt some more songs if you want to be a *diva*.'

'No, no, no,' she screamed, stamping her little foot. Mr. Lindoe glanced anxiously towards the stage and swept her away. Business was not so good that he could risk his patrons' displeasure. He'd heard that Master Wordsworth was drawing the crowds at his father's entertainments in a rival Norwich establishment.

'But I *like* being little Bess.'

'And you will learn to like 'Babes in the Wood' too or you shall soon see the back of my hand. And you don't want to be ousted by that whipper-snapper of a boy.'

'Indeed not. Anyway, boys cannot sing *my* songs.'

'Mama shall make you another ragged gown for 'The Begging Gypsy',' he wheedled. He could deny his only child nothing.

*****

Before long, Master Wordsworth was performing sonatas on the Grand Pianoforté. Lucy was too small for that, but not to be out beaten, Mr. Lindoe purchased a diminutive harp and she made such good progress that the crowds soon returned.

The rivalry between the two families continued to grow as did their children. Lucy swore she hated Master Wordsworth, but one night they were both appearing at the Vauxhall Gardens in Norwich, he in the Pavilion, she in the Pantheon. Bored with the plays, and stifled by the heat of the candles, they each sneaked out to take the air and drink tea in the gloaming. By chance, they entered the same booth, and got into conversation, at first without recognition. They were charmed with each other's company, and thereafter met secretly to whisper sweet nothings. Joseph even gave Lucy a silver ring as a token of his eternal love. In public, to humour their fathers, they continued to spar.

One summer, by special desire of the Countess of Bedfordshire, it was agreed that the child prodigies should appear together in a benefit concert. Lucy dressed more carefully than usual, becoming quite the fine lady although only ten. They sang together like angels, duet versions of Tom Moore's *Irish*

Melodies. The audience roared, demanding encore after encore, 'The Harp that once through Tara's Halls,' 'The Last Rose of Summer.' The fathers toasted each other in gin.

Then it happened. At the climax of the 'The Minstrel Boy', Joseph opened his mouth for the high note, and nothing came out. He looked round anxiously, as if wondering where top G had gone to. Lucy looked daggers, but held on to her own part to cover the lapse. He opened his mouth again, but there was only a croak. Covered in confusion, red as a turkey cock, he stood there miming till it was over, then slunk off to hide.

Enraged, Lucy tracked him down. He was sitting in a dark corner, head between his knees, actually weeping with shame and frustration.

'How could you!' she screamed. 'Call yourself a musician and you make that dreadful noise. I shall never sing with you again. Ever.'

'But Lucy,' he croaked in vain.

'I'll never even speak to you again. Take this,' and she tore the ring from the shallows of her bosom, hurled it at him and stamped off in high dudgeon.

Poor Joseph never sang a note again—his man's voice was disappointingly thin and although competent, he felt too humiliated to perform.

*****

The years passed, and Lucy, having an artistic temperament, did indeed become a diva and was all the rage in London and Bath. The name Lucy Lindoe became a magnet drawing the highest in the land to hear the 'Norfolk Canary.' At the height of her fame, she attracted the eye of a peer of the realm, who installed her as his mistress in a small mansion near Great Baddenham in the depths of Suffolk. When lordly duties allowed, they lived together very happily and she bore him many children. In time, she called in a visiting music master to instruct them on the pianoforté. She herself taught them singing and the girls the harp, for her lord liked to gaze at her playing so elegantly.

After the first session of lessons, Madame went to the music room herself to examine M. Le Bon Mot and the children's progress. He spoke of fingering and natural good taste and Mr. Hook's *Sonatinos for the use of Scholars*.

As he continued, Madame caught a familiar intonation in his voice, and eyed him thoughtfully.

'I seem to know you Monsieur. Have we not sung together in the past?' He looked up, met her eye, and blushed as red as a turkey cock.

'Lucy Lindoe!'

'Joseph Wordsworth!' they chorused, seeing through the disguises of their changed names and circumstances as they fell into each other's arms.

She kept her word about never singing with him again, as he had entirely given up the art of song, but as lordly duties allowed, which they increasingly did, he was frequently to be found by her side, and they certainly were on speaking terms.

Miss Lindoe and Master Wordsworth, whose fathers were rival impresarios, were child prodigies in Norwich around 1800. Both children performed in the same programme at least once, although the events of this story are invented. As far as I know, there was no 'Norfolk Canary,' although a series of song-books was published using other bird names in the title.

THERE'S NONE SO DEAF

Hilda Reynolds, Mrs, was the undisputed Queen of the Urn in Little Baddenham, everyone said so. No coffee morning, sale, tea party nor Sunday Service was complete without her presiding over the hot drinks. Having been in catering all her working life, and a volunteer helper-out for as long as she could remember, she, naturally, took over when old Mrs Cruickshank moved away. Hilda enjoyed being a Pillar of Society much better than doing school dinners at St Edmund's C of E Primary. The whole town depended on her, and no one looked down on her at all.

Hilda liked doing the Coffee after Church best. The stand-pipe was outside the north door and, before Service, she had to get one of the few Strong Men to help carry the heavy urn from the tap to the south transept. Being a widow, she got quite a thrill from the Strong Men even though they were all married. Then, during Service, she had to creep up to the front to See to the Urn in case it was over-boiling or not switched on properly. She walked as quietly as she could, but even so everybody turned their heads to look at her, so she always dressed smartly and wore her best high heels.

'Coffee or tea and welcome to St Edmund's,' she'd say to strangers, though she knew the regular congregation's needs better than they did themselves. And they thanked her so profusely she felt quite the gracious lady.

Then, one day, just before Easter, Ted, one of the Church Wardens, spoke to her, looking a bit embarrassed.

'Don't think we're not grateful for your sterling work, Hilda, but there have been some — er — complaints.'

'Beg pardon?' That Ted, his voice was ever so quiet. Hilda bristled all over once he spoke up.

'Not about my refreshments I hope!'

'Indeed not. No one could possibly fault your excellent brews. You're a tower of strength. No, it's just that some people find the sound of your — er — footsteps distracts them from worship.'

'No need to shout, I may be getting a bit hard of hearing but I'm not deaf yet. I have to Check the Urn. If Some People feel like that, then they can jolly well do it themselves. And if you think I'm going to get one of them hearing aids, it'll be over my dead body. So There!'

Noisy footsteps indeed! No cat could walk more quietly. They'd just said it out of spite.

Hilda stomped out.

*****

As the weeks passed, Hilda took to dropping in on town functions to gloat over how badly the well-heeled ladies were coping with the catering without her.

'Won't you return to your duties, Hilda, my dear?' they gushed. 'We can't fill the rota with anyone half as competent as you.'

But Hilda stuck to her guns. She knew when she wasn't wanted, and unless they apologised...

There was a raffle at the Age Concern coffee morning. Hilda hovered, admiring the many prizes: toiletries, bottles of wine, a crystal vase that would look ever so nice on her windowsill. You could tell Some People had donated Christmas presents they hadn't liked. Ungrateful or what. She was about to poke into a posh shoe-box, Echos they were, when Mrs Loveday, the Vicar's wife bore down on her. She had a nice clear voice, a bit la-di-da though.

'Only a pound a strip, and you're bound to win something since there are so many prizes.'

Hilda stumped up a whole fiver, after all it was for a Good Cause.

She got in a right old flutter while the Vicar was calling out the winners. Green 342, yellow 215... Her number was the very last. Oh dear, someone had beaten her to it for the vase, only the shoes remained. She sniffed, then brightened.

'Fancy that,' they're exactly my size. It must of been Meant.'

'Lovely soft leather and ever so comfortable,' said Mrs Loveday, 'I have a pair myself—such good quality, better even than Padders, and quite smart enough for church, even if they're flat heeled.'

*****

Whenever Hilda now strode up for Communion, no-one glared at her at all.

Then, the week before Whit Sunday, Fred, her favourite Strong Man, sidled up to her after Service.

'Beg pardon,' she said as soon as he started speaking, Fred, he had such a quiet voice. If only he would use that microphone thingy like the Clergy.

'Now you've taken to wearing quiet shoes, we were all wondering if you would consider resuming your duties at the urn. We would be so grateful…'

Hilda was all over smiles when she at last understood.

*****

Time passed, and they were all talking about a massive fund-raising effort to improve the Facilities of the church. The Vicar spoke about it in his Sermon.

'St Edmund's is a medieval building of enormous historical importance, but hitherto there have been no Facilities at all, apart from the outside tap. History does not record the capacity of medieval bladders but it must have been pretty large, unless folk used the churchyard or lived nearby.'

Some People tittered. Hilda snorted. It was so Unseemly for People in Holy Orders to be so coarse.

'After lengthy debate, St Edmund's has been granted permission to modify the area under the tower to provide a kitchen. The adjoining clergy-vestry will be converted to house able-bodied and disabled toilets.'

That's Little Baddenham

Hilda's heckles rose. She'd have to put them right about Health and Safety.

*****

There were more sales and coffee mornings than ever, so Hilda's services were in even greater demand. The great day came when the fund-raising was complete. Ted, the Church Warden, announced the winner of the sponsored tea drinking. It was a good thing he used that microphone thingy.

'This challenge has proved incontrovertibly just how much Facilities in the church are needed. And the winner is, not surprisingly, our very own Reverend David Loveday, who totted up the most cups of tea, followed closely by Reverend Adam Godly, our curate.'

'I could of told you who would win,' Hilda whispered behind her hand to her friend, Norma.

For weeks, Hilda and her Urn were on call non-stop, while the Strong Men helped the contractors dig trenches and partition the tower room. They even asked her opinion on the layout of the kitchen, well, more a kitchenette really.

When all the work was done, Hilda proudly took possession of her domain. She'd now be able to sit in her pew at the back, wearing her soft shoes, and creep into the tower room to See to the Urn, while everyone worshipped in peace. Pity she'd no longer need the services of a Strong Man... Howsumever, she'd still dress smartly…

She'd often wondered why the choir-stalls were at the back. In most churches, the Choir sat in the Chancel, near the Altar, but not St Edmund's. Them

St Edmund's folk were always contrary, as she well knew. When it was time to go up for Communion, the Organist came down from the organ loft in his robes to lead the choir up the front.

Why on earth did Organ-Morgan made such a song and dance about opening and closing that door to the tower? It wasn't as if it stuck or anything. Sometimes he turned and wagged his finger at it like it was a naughty choirboy. Or girl, not that there were many kiddies in the choir these days... Not at all suitable behaviour for an Organist. Sometimes, he would catch Sophie Loveday's eye, she was the Vicar's daughter and Head Chorister. He'd shrug his shoulders and cast up his eyes to heaven. She sometime wondered if he were a ha'penny short of a shilling.

*****

At the first Service after the makeover, there were cakes as well as biscuits, a right old jollification. Everyone always said nice things about Hilda's coffee and walnut and Victoria sponge. As soon as the choir had finished the anthem, she got up and opened the door into the tower room to See to the Urn. Everything was in order, but when she came out, that Sophie Loveday was shushing and waving her arms around wildly. Young People these days had no manners at all. Hilda strode back to her pew. Why on earth was everyone looking at her like that?

Then she saw Sophie deep in conversation with Fred, her favourite Strong Man. Perhaps it was something to do with the bells. She was just wiping down the worktop when he sidled up to her.

'Lovely coffee and walnut, Hilda my dear.'

'Beg pardon, can't you speak up.'

He did, bellowed for the whole congregation to hear. 'That latch clangs ferociously, and it's almost impossible to stop the door slamming. Complaints from the congregation, alas, are raising their ugly heads once more.'

'No need to shout Fred, I may be getting a bit hard of hearing, but I'm not deaf yet.'

'I understand the wicked ways of that door pretty well so, in future, could you possibly wait to attend to the urn till I open it to ring the bell for the Our Father?'

'Or me,' put in Sophie, shouting into Hilda's ear. 'And make sure you wait to be escorted back into the church.'

*****

Everyone was smiles, once more, that is, until the Summer Series. Hilda had never heard of a Summer Series until she read about it in the East Anglian Daily Times.

> *'Sir Reuben Goldberg OBE, the world famous conductor, has retired to Little Baddenham, where his brother Leo, Emeritus Professor of Music, has lived for several years. Not so long ago, Leo's children, Jacob and Rachel used to delight us with recitals at St Edmund's.*
>
> *Sir Reuben has been delving into Little Baddenham parish records and has made a remarkable discovery.*
>
> *'I have come upon irrefutable evidence that a renowned composer, one Thomas Mallis, breathed his first in this very village. We must have our very own Festival for the Quartercenary and put Little Baddenham on the*

musical map. Aldeburgh needn't think it's got a cultural monopoly of the entire Eastern Region.'

*****

Of course there had to be lavish teas, included in the price. The Vicar's wife bore down on Hilda, a pity she sometimes dropped her nice clear voice.

'*Look East* are coming to film the preparations. You're going to be on TV,'

'Beg pardon? That's right, I'll be doing the Teas,' Hilda agreed, putting down the shrugged shoulders and telling upwards glances to vicious spite.

Now Fred, he didn't hold with concerts so didn't show up. On the first afternoon of the Summer Series, Hilda, dressed up to the nines, sat in her usual place. The choir, it seemed, had come all the way from some Cambridge college. Hilda had no idea what they were singing about. It all sounded very distant and distorted, not a bit like when the kiddies used to sing at school concerts. Come to think, St Edmund's choir sometimes sang Foreign stuff like that, though why they couldn't sing in plain English she'd never know. As the clock struck the half hour, Hilda swept across the back of the church to Do the Urn for half time.

*****

That Sophie Loveday, she was sitting in her usual place in the choir-stalls looking totally blown away. Perhaps she was On Something. Suddenly, as Hilda put up the latch, Sophie began pointing to the door and making shushing signs. Then they were all at it, but Hilda had her job to do. When she flung up the kitchen hatch, she saw the conductor turn round and gawp at her. His arm stopped waving and about time too. Good thing the Urn was steaming away exactly as it should. As the singing started again, she removed cling-film and foil wrappings to reveal a mouth-watering display of cakes on the trolley all ready to push out. St Edmund's choir never broke down like that. Most unprofessional. As the clapping died down, she was ready with her mammoth teapot and jugs of hot water on the hatch. Everyone was strangely silent as she poured away with her usual greeting. 'Tea or coffee and welcome to St Edmund's, help yourself to cake. I can recommend the lemon drizzle.' Their response was far from gracious, in fact Hilda reckoned they were downright rude.

'Could you open the door more quietly, please' they bawled. 'Banging like that ruined the music.' Some of them, even Sir Reuben himself, tried saying it louder, and louder, and making rude gestures as if she was Foreign, but she smiled on.

Fed and watered, the audience returned to their seats as Hilda wheeled the trolley back into the tower room. Good thing it had stopped squeaking. She decided do a bit of washing up and save the other ladies the trouble afterwards. She tied on her best pink apron, ready to stack the dirty crockery into the dishwasher.

'Hold you hard, Missus, thou should'st not be adoing that right now.'

An elderly clergyman in a long black robe and a squarish sort of hat was writing at a tall sloping desk. He was holding a big feather thingy.

'Sound do carry, even if thou can'st not hear it, and thy racketing about be most noisome.'

Hilda's reflex 'beg pardon' was un-necessary. She was amazed at how loudly he spoke, he didn't sound hoity-toity like Some Folk even if he talked a bit like the old Prayer Book. For once, every word was crystal clear.

'No need to shout,' she replied. 'I may be getting a bit hard of hearing, but I'm not deaf yet. What's more, I wouldn't be seen dead in one of them hearing aids.'

The stranger cleared his throat. 'Ah, but there are none so deaf as those who will not hear.'

'But I can hear you as clear as a bell.'

'But do thou think on how much richer thy life would be if thou could'st but hear.'

Hilda gawped, lost for words.

'Thine heart might be in the right place, but thou provokest much wrath and indignation with thine infernal noise. When they do attempt to enlighten thee, thou can'st not hear their words of wisdom and kindness. Do thou listen.

'When I was priest in this parish, my first baptism was of a young boy, one Thomas Mallis, whose voice, when he grew older, would have moved the hearts of angels. His family being poor, I had him sent to London to become a singing boy at St Paul's from whence he rose to become Master of the Choristers and the greatest composer of his time. But alas, Thomas, at the pinnacle of his powers, he was stricken with deafness. Imagine, though he could pen what was in his mind's ear, he could listen no more to his sublime music. He would have given the world to regain his hearing, but alas, in the days of yore, there was no cure for his affliction. But now, by some miracle, the lame may walk, the blind may see and the deaf may hear. Yet in thy stubbornness and vain pride, thou refusest the aid that is at hand.'

Hilda could feel tears of misery dribbling down her face, she was blushing she was sure.

'So that's what they were saying! Oh, if only I'd known!'

The old priest led her to the tower door, and noiselessly opened it a crack. 'Listen! Do thou listen to the sad soaring music echoing around the vaulted roof. Is't not sublime?'

Hilda did listen, moved as she'd never been moved before. Every word was clear. 'Mallis is dead, Mallis is dead…'

She heard the silence, and was nearly deafened by the applause as the old man drew her back into the tower room.

'Do thou slip out of the West Tower door and make thy peace on the morrow.' He held up his hand in blessing.

'Thanks a million Vicar. I'll now see about getting one of them hearing aids.'

It wasn't until she was outside, breathing in the sweet smell of newly mown grass, that Hilda remembered the door she had just walked through had been sealed up in olden times.

No Second Fiddle

'Why can't you put *me* in for Young Musician of the Year too?' whinged Rachel, her fingers *glissandoing* up and down the keyboard with great panache to make her point. 'After all, Jake is only 12. I'll be too old next time.'

'No, no, no, and a thousand times no. You're competent, you're good, excellent even, but Jacob is something special, a genius, and his youthfulness will go in his favour. He needs this exposure, and think of the glory you'll get as his accompanist — not some stuffy old professor like me, but a vibrant young girl.'

'But it's not fair, Pa. I'm just as good, and I'm ten times more conscientious.' It was a flashy *arpeggio* this time. 'While I'm doing serious practice, he's forever messing about with improvisations and music paper.'

'No. The logistics of ferrying one of you around now we live in the sticks are bad enough, but both of you...'

'That's total rubbish Pa. And you're putting him in for two classes, violin *and* piano. I tell you what, it's because I'm a girl. You're nothing but a male chauvinist pig.'

Leo's deep brown eyes steeled, but he refused to be drawn.

Rachel flounced around in a permanent huff and complained to her old Austrian Grandmother, and all her friends, but she was really fond of her little brother, and began honing her accompaniment skills. She was endlessly patient in prising Jake out of his bedroom, where each and every wall was festooned with certificates, posters, cups and various awards proclaiming his precocious genius.

'Come on Jake, we must practice the *adagio* again. You get so carried away with the *rubato* it's impossible to synchronise. No, stop scribbling and pay attention. And that bubble gum's disgusting!' She snatched his pen from his hand, in so doing leaving an unseemly mark on the intricately covered manuscript paper.

'How dare you spoil my masterpiece, it's ruined now.' He pulled the sticky mess lugubriously backwards and forwards from his mouth.

'You know very well it's not, because it's all in your head.'

Jake discarded the offending gum, grinned disarmingly, and rushed off to the music room to demonstrate his latest creation at the grand piano.

'Don't you think I'll get credit for composing the contemporary work myself?'

Rachel poked him in the ribs. 'Dunno, but I'm quite sure you won't let the adjudicators overlook it!'

*****

'You shouldn't be too hard on your father, *leibling,*' pleaded Grandmother one day over the washing up. 'It was so hard for him to accept that his accident permanently put paid to his performing career.'

'Indeed, it wasn't easy to see his brother outshine him so publicly,' put in Ma. 'Sir Reuben Goldberg OBE is a hard act to compete with. Your father sees teaching, even at the Royal College, as a bit of a come-down you know. To compensate, he puts all his energies into encouraging you two.'

'Slave-driving more like. It's always, "and how many hours have you practised today?" And Jake's *way* behind with his education. He's practically illiterate if not dyslexic. At least I go to school.'

Her mother sighed. 'Little Baddenham College is a very good school with a strong musical tradition. That's why we moved here, so you could attend as day-pupils and have the advantage of your father's help as well. And St Edmund's has such a wonderful acoustic for your recitals. But Rachel, you mustn't blame your father if he wants to live out his dreams through Jacob.'

'Even if it means taking a back seat, *leibling.*'

Grandmother hung up the tea towel.

'And he's never really got over having his application for Principal of the RCM being rejected.'

'Get out the violins. All he wants is to bask in borrowed glory.' Rachel stomped off muttering about discrimination and Women's Lib.

*****

A few days later, Rachel just happened to overhear a seminal snatch of conversation between Grandmother and her father.

'You're not being fair to the girl Leo, you know you're not. When I think of all the sacrifices your father and I made, giving you both music lessons when we had nothing, nothing, I say, after we fled to England as refugees. If it's the money, I'll pay, I've a little put by.'

So Rachel was entered for the piano class. She was overjoyed and when not practising spent her limited spare time going round the shops in Norwich with her friends to choose The Dress in case she got through to the final rounds.

As for Jake, he warmly congratulated his sister on their father's change of heart.

'Cool! You'll get into the semi-final, Sis, no sweat, but make sure you don't beat me!'

*****

The trailing around, competing and judging continued for months, and the whole family grew frazzled as the children vied with each other for their father's advice and practice time on the grand piano. Eventually both got into their respective finals. As Leo had predicted, much was made of the brother-sister double act in the violin sonata class, and the media, as ever, played on the family theme.

'Talented duo…' 'No second fiddle for Rachel!' 'Blessed pair of prodigies!' 'Proud father puts down success to natural genius combined with discipline and hard work.'

*****

The string finals came first. Jake was supremely confident. 'Did you ever hear such crap?' he asked the TV interviewer, referring to a rival. 'Why, that wanker can't even play in tune.'

Watching the monitor in the green-room, Rachel winced and winced again, then exhaled deeply when the interviewer diverted him into telling them how his first public performance had been age four. *Grr!*

'Wasn't that rather unusual Jacob?'

'No, not really. I mean, I was pretty good, and Pa was dead set on it.'

'You don't think your father was too pushing?'

'Oh no, I loved every minute of it. Music is my whole life.'

'And do you think the family equilibrium will survive the sibling rivalry in the keyboard class?'

'No problem, everyone knows I'm better than my sister.'

Rachel struggled to regain her composure.

*****

Then they were on. Rachel surpassed herself, sensitive to every nuance of Jake's violin playing, and he executed a Bach unaccompanied sonata with mind-boggling virtuosity. When it came to the concerto of his own composition, everyone smiled and clapped and congratulated him on his performance, even Uncle Reuben. Leo was lapping up the euphoria.

'Think about the recording contracts…'

Jake won, of course.

*****

Then came the piano final.

'In third place, Thomas Linley.' Jake had become good mates with Tomo as they'd sat around between takes, endlessly chewing gum and making paper darts embellished with variants of Jake's name.

'Well done — I'm really pleased you've beaten my stuck-up sister.'

Rachel looked daggers.

'In second place, Jacob Goldberg.' Jake blanched into a cold sweat and seemed even smaller than he was.

'And in first place, Rachel Goldberg.'

Rachel glowed as she stepped forward in that oh-so-glorious dress to receive her award. She glanced round to catch her brother's eye, but he'd slunk off.

*****

At last came the final play-off for the coveted title of Young Musician of the Year. More nail biting, gum chewing, suspense, sycophantic smiles and yet another new dress. Uncle Reuben conducted the orchestra in the *Concerto* Class.

The finalists sat nervously on the platform as the judges mulled over their fates.

'And in a close second place, Jacob Goldberg, violin.

'And this year's winner is, Rachel Goldberg, piano.' The applause and hugging and kissing were overwhelming.

*****

Down came the posters and certificates; away went the piles of manuscript; the cups tarnished in a cupboard; the violin case lay unopened, and Jake brooded and sulked and raged. His voice broke and he exhibited the worst possible teenage behaviour.

His parents were in despair.

'He was always such a happy child,' bemoaned his mother.

'So much wasted talent,' complained his father, 'and after all we've spent on him.'

'You've brought it on yourself, son,' said Grandmother as she knitted away in her corner. 'You pushed him too hard, he never had a chance to be a normal child.'

Psychologists and psychiatrists were consulted, to little effect. Even within the hallowed walls of a private sector school, Jake failed miserably in mainstream education. He truanted, scraped a few GCSEs, then disappeared off the face of the earth.

*****

Rachel flourished as a concert pianist, travelling world-wide with orchestras and giving intimate recitals in prestigious venues, not forgetting to honour the townsfolk of Little Baddenham. The traumatic experience of her brother's disappearance only added depth to her performance.

'It's all my fault,' she'd sob. 'If only I hadn't insisted on entering that silly competition, he wouldn't have done this.'

'Don't be so hard on yourself,' said her mother.'

'You had to be true to your talent, *leibling*,' said her grandmother.

'No, no, the fault is mine,' sighed her father, beating his chest with the stub of his index finger. 'I shouldn't have pushed him so hard, no wonder he cracked up.'

Leo's dark curls greyed with worry as his wife clucked and fussed over him, every day missing her darling boy. The old Austrian grandmother faded and eventually died.

*****

Soon after this sad event, the family *Sabbat* dinner was disturbed by a knock on the door.

'Whoever can it be? I'll go.' Rachel clattered down her cutlery.

'Good God!' On the threshold was a bedraggled, face-fungussed, dreadlocked monster, with blood-shot eyes rolling out of his head. Behind him floated a shadowy waif clutching a guitar case.

'Hi Sis.' He threw down a tattered back-pack.

Rachel ushered them into the dining room, where his parents strove to reconcile their feelings of shock mingled with relief.

'Jacob, welcome home!' said Leo.

'My darling boy,' said his mother, embracing him.

The girl sported a pregnant bulge when she put down the guitar.

'I've had enough of sex, drugs and rock'n' roll,' Jake muttered. 'Mel won't marry me unless I get clean, so we've come home, that is if you'll have us. It's going to be a long struggle.'

'First things first, a hot bath, clean clothes then food,' pronounced Mother. 'We're just finishing, there's plenty of chicken soup and salmon, I'll just do a few more veg while you sort yourselves out.'

*****

'But what have you been doing all these years, son?' asked Leo later.

'Didn't you know we'd be worried sick about you?' said Ma.

'It wouldn't have hurt to pick up the phone.' Rachel's guilty feelings made her uneasy.

'But you must have seen me in the charts, heard gigs on Radio 1.'

The parents looked puzzled.

'But we don't even know how to tune in to Radio One.'

'I never follow the charts,' confessed Rachel. 'We don't do pop music here.'

*****

Through the long rehab, the family tried obliquely to encourage Jake to resume his old love of classical music.

'It's no good, I'm not going back to that crap, Sis! Stuff like *Eine Kleine Nachtmusik's* only fit for call centres. But just you wait and see what we've got up our sleeves,' he'd say, jigging the baby up and down.

*****

Rachel, with her host of friends and useful contacts, eventually got him going, in spite of her gruelling schedule.

Five years on, Jake's name was up in dazzling lasers in the West End, as was his adoring wife's as his lead singer. Rave reviews of *Sunlight Espresso* appeared in music magazines and in both the tabloid and broad-sheet press. Songs from the show went out on every wavelength the world over as a totally new concept in rave rock-opera was revealed.

'The first of many,' crowed the young Maestro on the opening night as Mel was taking the umpteenth curtain call. Wet-eyed but smiling, Rachel turned proudly to her father, who was rubbing his hands in glee at the thought of all the royalties.

'Pa, this will checkmate Lord Floyd-Webber for all time!'

'Inevitably, my dear!'

A Tooth for a Tooth

Hilary Frederica Pierce was a ghoulish child from the start. When given a nurse's set for her fifth birthday, instead of bandaging and tucking up sick dollies, she took to operating on perfectly sound soft toys. When her mother remonstrated, Freddy protested that she was practising to be a surgeon.

'Little girls can't be surgeons.'

'But I won't be a little girl when I grow up.'

'True enough, but it's not at all suitable.'

'Why?'

Mummy scratched her head. 'Well, for a start. You haven't got the right clothes. Surgeons wear a green gown and a mask.'

Further inspections of forbidden television programmes proved this to be true. Hunting through the jumble sale pile, Freddy was highly delighted to discover some shirts approximating to clinical green. Next time the vet called to attend an ailing ewe, Freddy hid behind some bales of hay in the barn until she had a chance to slip out and appropriate a mask from his bag. Thus armed, she progressed from dismembering furry toys to dissecting the little dead animals the cats brought in and amputating limbs from her big sisters' long cast off dolls.

When Freddy's mother, hoping for support, reported this unladylike behaviour to her husband, a bull-headed farmer, he laughed uproariously.

'Shows a lot of spunk for a girl.'

After four nearly grown up daughters, Freddy's father had yearned for a boy to take over the farm, and to compensate for his disappointment had insisted the little afterthought be given a more or less unisex name. When Freddy was eight, he took her out hunting, shooting and fishing, delighting in her prowess and lack of squeamishness when blooded. At ten, she was allowed to help with the lambing, and by twelve, it was generally assumed that she had cast off her infant aspirations to butcher humankind and would become a vet. Mummy envisaged her in a smart small-animal practice, while Daddy was convinced she would become his right-hand man with the stock.

In the secretness of her bedroom, Freddy accumulated a growing collection of skeletal parts she had gleaned from her heathland walks: sheep's thigh bones, birds' breasts, rabbit heads, and once a whole dog with innumerable teeth, stuck, no doubt, down a rabbit hole newly exposed by an uprooted tree.

*****

Grandad's false teeth clicked dreadfully, so much so that Freddy made any excuse to cut short her visits to the barn conversion that failed miserably to accommodate her grandparents' homely life style.

'My teeth are as good as new,' Grandma would boast. 'They're the oldest part of me. Every other cell in my body's changed over and over, but I've had the same teeth for seventy years. Not like some I could name who never looked after them and need new ones.'

And Grandad would sit with his muddy boots on, obliviously sucking at his smelly pipe and interminably clicking his teeth.

When Freddy was fourteen, her apple-cheeked grandmother, who had never known a day's illness in her life, had a heart attack and died. They rented out their barn conversion and Grandad moved back into the old farmhouse with them, listlessly fumigating the chimney corner all day and every day.

How those teeth grated: *Click, click, click* when he spoke; *click, click, click,* when he chewed; *click, click, click* even when he snored or cleared his throat. Every nerve lacerated, Freddy turned into one long walking mood. She dropped hints, she threatened, she shouted, but to no avail. Grandad persisted in not getting new teeth, and her parents' demands that she be kind to the poor old man fell on deaf ears. His only sop was to occasionally remove the offending dentures altogether and enquire sibilantly whether his toothless state suited her any better. If anything, this was worse. It turned him from a generally jolly old boy into a whining old crone.

One day, Freddy found a complete skull, human she was almost sure. She wasn't concerned about whether it was of interest to archaeologists or the police, but worked the jawbone, chomped the imperfect teeth, gave voice to the long-dead tongue.

'Death comes to us all old man, but mark my words, if you don't get some new teeth, I'll strike you dead and see that you suffer aeons of toothache in expiation for the agony you inflict daily on your nearest and dearest. Cursed be they that neglect their teeth!'

Freddy decided to make up sets of teeth from the bones in her possession, searching frenetically for yet more to complete the collection. She examined each find for imperfections; from jagged holes, she gauged the degree of pain suffered by the deceased; guessed at the cause of a tooth split in half or shaped awry. She consulted library books, and became an expert in tooth detection. Herbivore, carnivore, omnivore, age, you could tell it all from the teeth, and still no cure for Grandad's gnawing habit. Freddy's investigations took a practical turn. She acquired a miniature vice, clamped in an errant tooth, and with the smallest drill bit she could find, she would methodically extirpate the furthest corner of the decay. As she drilled, tongue stuck out in concentration, she vicariously punished her hapless grandparent, viciously inflicting the maximum pain for his sins of omission.

By the time she was sixteen, Freddy knew that she must become not a surgeon, nor a vet, but a dentist. Her mission was twofold: to get her own back on all neglecters of teeth; and to ensure, by proper dental care and education, that no-one had to endure the torture of clicking teeth ever again.

Suddenly, teeth were everywhere: a body charred beyond recognition identified by its dental records; a corpse buried in a forest turned skeleton likewise; a murder victim whose face had been pulped beyond recognition. Freddy wondered if they had a special branch of dentistry to deal with forensics and longed to join it. She imagined the power of such a position: the power to prove identity beyond all shadow of a doubt, and thus let the loved ones grieve; the power to promote justice — the murderer tracked down and punished, or an innocent suspect reprieved through establishing the connection between person, place and time.

'What A-levels do I need for dentistry?' she asked her teacher at Little Baddenham High School where she was bussed from the Sandlings side of the A12. When she informed her parents of her changed career plans, her father was none too pleased, but Mummy thought it an improvement on large animal vetinary practice.

For seven long years, she nursed her ambition to become the world's leading forensic dentist and patiently drilled, filled and extracted artificial, then real teeth, sculpted dentures and made photo fits from dental records on the side. And still Grandad's teeth clicked horrendously, though she seldom had to grin and bear it since she mostly lived with her boyfriend, judiciously chosen as he intended to become a top CID man.

The year she qualified, Grandad died, and she fell pregnant. To distract herself between bouts of morning sickness, she consumed vast quantities of crime fiction and all her husband's professional journals.

The day the youngest of her four children started school, she resumed her postponed career, initially in normal practice. Though the senior partner congratulated her on her success with preventative care and made her tempting offers of advancement, she insisted on applying for a course in forensics. Soon she would be able to fulfil her dream of dispensing justice and retribution.

Although several fires and air crashes occurred while she was studying, she found the identification of charred bodies less than stimulating.

'The results are too predictable,' she complained to her professor. 'I find working on corpses in copses and heads battered beyond identification more challenging. Bite recognition is important in establishing guilt.'

The Professor had always considered her morbid interest curious.

'You'd better make the most of it then Freddy,' he joked. 'DNA testing will put most of us out of a job before long. It's fast becoming the primary method of detection you know.'

CRUICSHANK CHRONICLES III
RAMBLING ROSIE

Rosie Cruickshank was at last homeward bound. Like the white fluffy clouds whizzing past the portholes, events in her life skimmed muzzily by. Oh dear, she was getting maudlin after quantities of not very cool white wine served from nasty little airline bottles.

Stuffy old Julian and Tony had both left home by the time Pop had become ill, but sixteen had been a bad time for her to lose a parent after a horrible, lingering illness. No wonder she'd messed up her exams. Somehow, her life had never really got back on course...

What had possessed her to marry Sid? One night at a folk-singing pub, she'd caught the deep brown eyes of a hunk overflowing with Irish charm. It had been love at first sight. At school, she'd toyed with Women's Lib: she'd been fired with socialism, preaching emancipation and an end to class distinction. At the time, it had seemed romantic to marry a Working Class Man against everything her family held dear. Tony, had advised her to follow her heart. Her mother Laura, icily stoic, had made her wait till she was eighteen.

Predictably, it hadn't worked out. Rosie smiled wryly, as she recalled the night when, exasperated beyond reason at her husband's increasing drink habit, she'd stormed over to their insalubrious local, failed to draw Sid's attention from his beer-swilling mates, seized his half-empty pint, and tipped it over his head. Spluttering, he had hustled her out before she could vocalise her complaints in public.

'How can you prefer those louts to me?' she'd screamed. 'What would you say if I spent the equivalent of your beer and fags money on Cultural Activities?'

When things had starting falling apart, she'd frequently confided in Tony before crashing out on his sofa.

'He's so coarse! We've nothing in common…'

'I thought you said he comes along to your Drama Club.'

'That doesn't count, it's only because he's doing the lighting. Qualified electricians that work for free are hard to come by.'

They'd struggled on for a while then started divorce proceedings without too many hard feelings. At least, there had been no children to complicate matters.

Rosie had braved the 'I told you so's' and caustic remarks about making her own bed and lying in it, and gone home to her mother's, briefly—she'd always loved Orchard Place. When Laura demanded she pay her way, she'd been astounded.

'You've got loads of money Ma,' she'd moaned, 'you've never begrudged me anything before, and you know what a state I'm in...' Muttering about the recession, Laura had remained adamant, so Rosie had earned a pittance helping out at the Antiques Centre — after her father's early death, a tenant had continued the business in the barn. When her divorce came through, Laura's hints that she should move on became compelling. There had been no big row with the family, but the niggling resentment had festered, so she'd packed her bags and stomped off to work her way round the world, falling in and out of love and employment as she went. She'd seldom contacted her family, bar sending the odd postcard from exotic places and large self-addressed parcels to be stored in the attics. Happy days.

The stewardess hovered, offering more drinks. 'Coffee, strong coffee, please.'

As the years rolled by, Little Baddenham, once sloughed off as being narrow, backward looking and restrictive, grew more charming in recollection. She was done with romance: Orchard Place, the one permanent home in her much-travelled life, called her.

'Will passengers please fasten their seat-belts, we will shortly be landing at Heathrow...' She checked her bum bag for her passport, checked for the umpteenth time that the ten years hadn't expired. Thank goodness she'd retained her maiden name through thick and thin.

*****

When she turned up at Orchard Place with her enormous backpack, it was to find a For Sale notice at the end of the drive. Her heart lurched, she came out in a cold sweat, sat down on the dry grass. Surely her mother hadn't died? She should never have stayed away so long…

But no, Ma was well, if a little lame, and invited the whole clan round for a barbecue under the pear tree to celebrate the prodigal's return. It was just like old times, with nephews and nieces cheerfully chasing around.

It was there that the family solicitor caught up with Rosie and handed her a stiff yellowish envelope. It was Auntie Joan, her mother's little sister, who had died suddenly while Rosie was travelling. She had left all her worldly goods to her niece. The news was totally unexpected, but a trawl through her memory unveiled childhood recollections. Aunt and niece, both youngest children, had been close.

'I've seen the way those big brothers of yours treat you, Rosie, one minute spoiling you rotten, just like your mother, the next minute bullying and teasing you. I'll see you right dear, Laura can look after the boys.'

Funny thing, memory. Fancy Auntie Joan keeping her word after all these years.

*****

Mother and daughter were sharing a pot of tea in the old farmhouse kitchen. Rosie loved the ancient Aga, the familiar clothes airer hanging high above it, draped with ghosts of school uniform.

'It's not just that silly fall that's made me give in to your brothers and agree to sell up, dear…'

'What happened?'

'I was picking pears over your father's grave. How was I to know the ladder was rotten?' They laughed companionably. 'Orchard Place is falling into rack and ruin, dear. I can't afford to keep it going. Black Monday hit me hard. Besides, it needs a large family to live here, not a selfish old woman like me. I'll be much better off in a smart new bungalow near Julian. And you can move into Joan's place.'

Norwich didn't appeal.

'Ma,' said Rosie hesitantly over breakfast a few days later. 'Has money always been tight? Is that why you stopped supporting me before I went away?'

'Good heavens no, dear. Is that what all the fuss was about? No, I just thought it was about time you learned to stand on your own two feet.'

'Really?' Rosie hugged her mother close, waves of relief surging over her.

'I'm older and wiser now, Ma,' she smiled.

*****

'Selling up the ancestral home is dire,' Rosie stormed at her brothers. 'Why can't one of you buy the other out?' Visiting their mother in the sticks was one thing, it seemed, but taking on the mouldering pile was not compatible with anyone's life style.

The solution, once it came to Rosie, was obvious. What was to stop her buying the outbuildings with her legacy? She'd turn the barn into a Craft Centre, selling local as well as exotic ware—during her travels, she'd discovered a delight in tribal arts and crafts, an enthusiasm for Fair Trade and the attics were already overflowing with her souvenirs. She had worldwide contacts… She glowed as she envisaged the old stable block converted into craft workshops, a snug cottage for herself, a coffee shop overflowing into the courtyard in summer. Letting the studios would provide income to cover lean months…

Her mother was delighted with the scheme.

'So good to keep a family toe in the old place.'

Her brothers were enthusiastic and withheld the barn and adjoining outbuildings from the sale. When pressed, they agreed a peppercorn price. Everything went her way: the existing tenancy had not long to run; her cousin Roger, who worked in Building Regulations, advised her about planning permissions, and the townsfolk and their councillors agreed that such a facility would benefit locals and tourists alike. Diggins and Son Builders were delighted to have largely indoor winter work. While camping out in the building site, she signed up for an Open University Access Course in Arts.

*****

The Treasure Trove did well. Hitherto, hordes of tourists had arrived in their cars and coach loads to visit the Grade One Listed Castle and Grade One listed St Edmund's Church, but once they had patronised the shops and food outlets, they had hitherto found Little Baddenham had little else to offer day trippers, but now there was a new attraction. Laura helped out occasionally, her sister-in-law

Avril had many contacts and her sister-in-law Barbara was an excellent crafts person and maker of jams and pickles. Rosie provided a play area, and employed part-time young mothers during the week and sixth-formers at weekends and in the school holidays. The local media praised her prowess and business boomed.

'You've found your milieu at last Sis,' Tony told her. 'How's the boy friends?'

Rosie pursed her lips. 'The only man in my life is Percy, and he's only a dog.'

*****

Rosie took to championing the underdog and local causes. She and her friends, old and new, would spends hours putting the world to rights, sipping cool Prosecco at The Crown, or Cappuccinos at the Dancing Goat. They got heated about the need for more double yellow lines and car-parks, and less new housing, all in the interests of maintaining the ambience of the old town. She wrote letters to the council, she wrote to the East Anglian Daily Times, she wrote to her MP, as did her friend Annabel, who lived in the most picturesque street in the town.

'Watch out,' said her brother Tony, 'you're getting as bad as Avril.' Their sister-in-law was a Pillar of Society in Great Baddenham and into everything.

Neither of her sisters-in-law would have deigned to be seen at a folk-club, but when a session started up at The Crown, Rosie embraced it with enthusiasm. She was flattered when a guy tried to chat her up with 'Ramblin' Rose,' but she wasn't really into Country and Western.

One summer night, the bar was vibrating with:
> And it's no, nay never…
> Will I play the wild rover…

She joined in the chorus lustily, recalling her own return to the family fold.

When it was her turn, she launched into a pastiche protest ditty she'd written.
> Where have all the green fields gone?...
> Gone to housing every one…

Out of the corner of her eye, she became aware of a stranger with tousled black hair whose deep blue eyes were boring into her own. Her pulse hadn't raced like this for ages... When she sat down, the hunk made glass raising motions and nodded towards the bar.

They didn't re-join the session after the interval, but took their drinks to the courtyard garden at the back. There was a tea light in a jar on the table, and a single red rose in a vase.

'I couldn'a agree more with the sentiments of your song,' he said. The man reached out and took her hand. His finger nails were caked with potter's clay, and he was overflowing with Scottish charm.

ILL-CONSIDERED TRIFLES

Alice Bingham, fifty something, plumpish, had always been an inveterate snapper-up of ill-considered trifles.

'Not "*ill*" but '"*un*"' habitually bemoaned her children whose English teacher at Little Baddenham High School was a purist. 'Misquoting Shakespeare is *so* embarrassing.'

Alice supposed she'd inherited her addiction from her father and its mis-nomenclature from her mother's disapproval. She sometimes wondered if her father had been having it off with the musty smelling ladies in funny hats who kept the junk shops of her childhood. Hard to imagine her father having sex with anyone...

An unexpected bargain was a bonus, but for Alice, like Autolycus, her mousing cat, the buzz was in the quest. Little Baddenham had only two charity shops, but summer Saturdays saw coffee mornings, jumble sales or antiques fairs nearly every week, besides the car boot at the annual Gala. She made frequent forays to neighbouring towns—Aldeburgh was famed for designer clothes. After all, one woman's cast-offs are another woman's Nearly New. How her father would have doted on charity shops!

When a friend admired a new outfit, Alice would brush off the compliment with 'Oh I got it from Oxfam!' Or Mind, or the Hospice Shop... 'I dress entirely from charity shops.'

'Oh, so do I,' they gushed over their Agas, taking pains to squash the Harrods carriers into the depths of the receptacle for recycling and dog poo bags.

From her teens, Alice had had a problem with buying clothes. She would spend long hours dreaming up the perfect garment, so nothing in the shops ever measured up. She supposed this influenced her mature bargain hunting. Under that pile of shabby jumble, there just might lurk the elusive dress of her dreams. Her habit drove her husband and her children spare. 'Come on,' they'd chorus, 'we haven't got all day. Anyone would think you suffer from Obsessive Compulsive Disorder.'

With her first pay cheque, Alice had furnished her flat from a Mrs Whotsit who stashed 'quality' used pieces into a barn in Debenham. Having bargained for the bare essentials, most of which she later stripped down and made entirely presentable, her eye had caught a gleam of glass buried in straw. Her fingers scrabbled to find smooth bands circling the neck of a decanter. Not a single decanter, but a pair. 'I'll let you have them cheap,' said Mrs Whotsit, 'since the stoppers don't match.'

Looking back, the search marked the start of her obsession, for unattached stoppers proved a rarity. Nevertheless, the decanters came out for sherry when she entertained. 'Sweet or dry?' she offered, revelling in the elegance, and hoping her guests were not experts.

Soon after she met Bernard, they found one stopper, of perfect style and fit. It seemed like an omen. They celebrated with Croft Original.

'Here's to us,' they toasted, 'and may our troubles be small ones.' On honeymoon, they discovered an identical stopper and their joy was complete.

When the children were small, the decanters were incarcerated in a cupboard and rarely came out. One Christmas, young Jess was entrusted with the 'sweet or dry' routine and disaster shattered a stopper. Alice could hardly contain her wrath and exuded cold sullenness much like her late mother. Back to the cupboard went the decanters, and the stopper search joined the unattainable quests for missing plates from Great Aunt Grace's dinner service, a teapot for her mother's Spode and the current fantasy garment.

When she delivered her son to his new university, she spied her stopper in the window of an obscure antique shop. Overjoyed, she floated in, chatted winsomely to the owner, and struck a bargain while Brian stood sullenly by. 'Isn't it about time you grew up', he scowled, 'you can't go on being a left-over hippy for ever.'

Back home, she crowed over her success but Bernard was not impressed.

'Not more bloody junk,' — his perennial complaint — 'you know perfectly well we've nowhere to display them.'

'And I've been asking you for years to put up a few shelves to house my treasures.'

Bernard glowered, slammed the door and went off to play with his computer.

*****

One day, Alice swept in from the auction at Campsea Ash with a few boxes of 'sundries' and a charming Edwardian display unit to boot. Bernard appeared to be in one of his rare good moods, and was prevailed upon to put it up.

Alice lovingly arranged her knick-knacks. Autolycus leapt up to investigate and the cabinet came crashing down, shedding its load into countless shards.

Then she noticed the raw plugs, flayed out.

'You used the wrong bloody raw plugs you fool!' she screamed up the stairs. 'These are for plasterboard, not solid walls.'

Bernard came down grinning foolishly.

'This is the last straw, you philistine yob,' Alice yelled between sobs. 'If those decanters are destroyed, it's a matter for divorce and about time too.'

*****

With the children gone and no husband to nag her, Alice expended her energy on car-booting in a big way further to feed her habit. When she acquired her Senior Bus Pass, she became expert in the timetables, and scoured every reachable town in Suffolk for bargains, indulging in coffee and cream cakes over the carrier bags since she hadn't spent out on petrol.

'But Mum, all that fat is *so* bad for your figure,' Jess would nag. 'It's about time you joined me at TRIM AND TREAT.'

At last, Alice's expertise proved mildly profitable. Her stall flourished on the car boot circuit and on Little Baddenham's Saturday Market. She offered regular clients a search service and charged top whack. Even Bernard would have been impressed.

*****

Jess announced her engagement.

'I'll have such fun looking for the perfect mother-of-the-bride outfit. I can just see it in my mind's eye...' pronounced her parent, looking misty-eyed.

'Why can't you go to Jarrolds in Norwich like everybody else?' urged Jess.

'You know perfectly well I always dress from charity shops. Besides, I have the expense of the wedding.'

'But we only want a simple do, and we're paying anyway.' Jess neglected to mention the hefty cheque her father had sent. 'We won't invite you if you insist on turning out like a bag lady.'

Eventually Jess wheedled her mother into going to Norwich to find a mutually acceptable outfit.

By the end of the day, no such garment had been found, but Jess had a pretty shrewd idea of what her mother had in mind: a silvery grey dress and jacket, shot through with all the blue and green colours of the rainbow.

*****

While Alice continued to haunt the classier end of her circuit, Jess investigated what her mother wrote off as 'posh shops.' At last she found what she was looking for, but gulped when she saw the price tag. She asked the manageress to set aside the outfit while she thought about it.

'But Brian,' she pleaded down the phone to her brother, and 'But Stuart,' to her fiancé, 'we've simply got to do something about it. Can't we subsidise it between us, to make her dream come true?'

They concocted a master plan. Scenting a sale, the manageress joined the conspiracy and they handed over their three cheques by way of good faith.

The following Saturday, Jess drove Alice to Norwich yet again.

'Look Mum, we didn't try in here,' said Jess, all innocence.

'Clothes in the window without price labels always cost the earth,' protested her mother as Jess frog-marched her into the shop. Forewarned by a text, the manageress was hanging garments on a bargain rail sporting 'slight seconds.'

'Oh,' gasped Alice as her eye caught the silvery sheen. 'Oh,' she gasped again, as she fingered the fabric lovingly, looking furtively for the size and the price tag.

'Such a bargain, a quarter of the normal price,' interjected the manageress, mentioning a famous designer. Alice quivered with elation.

'Go on Mum, it can't hurt to try it on,' Jess urged, encouraged by the manic gleam in her mother's eyes.

'I wonder whether she means the quarter's "of"' or "off"?' Jess giggled, poking her head into the fitting room. 'Wow Mum, this outfit's something else!'

'There's nothing wrong with it at all except that the buttons don't match,' enthused the manageress. 'It's a perfect fit Madam, really flattering for your figure. Alice stood back to admire herself in the long mirror.

'Go on Mum. It takes pounds off you, makes you look ten years younger.

From behind her mother's back, Jess winked at the manageress. 'Would madam like to try a hat?' Jess nodded enthusiastically.

'If you think I'm going to wear one of those fancy feather dusters spiked with antennae you can think again.' Jess cast her eyes to heaven. She followed her mother's gaze as it fell on a gleaming peacock creation. 'My dream hat,' she sighed.

'I'm afraid that item isn't in the Sale,' muttered the manageress.

'Go on Mum, treat yourself for once. You're worth it! And you won't even have to buy new buttons, you've got millions at home.' Jess recalled happy childhood hours getting out the Princess Anne's Wedding biscuit tin and sorting the buttons into sets, buttons lovingly rescued from clothes cast off for recycling. Her mother got out her Visa card.

'And I'll take the hat too.'

Jess texted her menfolk. 'Mission accomplished! And don't ever let her find out about eBay.'

*****

The search through the tin was disappointingly short. With gloved hands, Alice sewed on the perfect buttons, saving the original ones in case they came in handy. Then she hung up her prize on the door to admire it.

The wedding day dawned sunny and bright, and everyone complimented the bride and her mother on their gorgeous attire. Alice positively glowed. The first new garment she'd bought in years even attracted the attentions of an uncle of the bridegroom who turned out to be equally keen on car boot sales. At the celebration lunch in a modest Italian restaurant, disaster struck in the form of a glass of Chianti being tipped all down the jacket.

'O Mama Mia,' moaned the offending waitress, ineffectually mopping off the worst of the stain.

Alice rushed off to the cloakroom and plunged the jacket into cold water. 'Dry clean only' she read as she sloshed it around. Returning to the table, wounded bitterly, she tried to brush off the condolences. The restaurateurs were anxious to make amends, but the dream outfit turned out to be the end of a line and so irreplaceable.

'You can always wear the dress on its own,' urged Jess when she returned from honeymoon, but Alice could never bring herself to wear it again, not even for the first christening.

'The dress is too low cut,' she'd say, 'I'd freeze to death.'

But of course the hunt was on. With renewed vigour, she searched manically for the elusive part of her ruined dream: she was first to queue at every jumble sale or coffee morning; she arrived at car boot sales before the crack of dawn; she volunteered at the Hospice Shop so she could have first picking. She even joined Saga weekend bargain breaks, sometimes accompanied by Stuart's uncle Ben, so she could binge on tracking down her prey in far-away places.

Then it happened, one weekend in Cardiff. Taking a last minute wander before boarding the coach, she saw it in Age Concern. The identical jacket hung on a model wearing an entirely unsuitable skirt. Alice's adrenalin rush failed to budge the door—it was Sunday. She looked at her watch. Time to fly. Perhaps she should stay over, but the endless journey home by public transport was beyond her. Besides, Ben was taking her out to dinner next day. The outfit would be too posh for The Orangery, but you never know… She scrabbled feverishly in her handbag, scribbled a few words on the back of a receipt, stuffed it in an old envelope along with a ten pound note, posted it through the letter box and ran.

'Come on, we haven't got all day,' niggled the coach driver as he stowed her baggage.

*****

'What's this then Gladys?' The well-rounded Age Concern manageress conferred with her assistant over the torn envelope next morning. 'I do 'ope she knows what she's axsing for. She'd need to be an anorexic bean pole to fit this, like!'

'No 'arm in sending it off is there? After all, she's paid good money.'

GREAT
—I DON'T KNOW HOW MANY TIMES GREAT— AUNT LIZZIE'S WEDDING GOWN

Louise sat in her car, watching a gaggle of females sidling furtively into Little Baddenham Village Hall. The fat ones overflowed their clothes, all bosom and belly, while the thin ones' clothes flapped gauntly. When the door finally cut out the shrill chatter, Louise discreetly inspected the bill board: 'TRIM AND TREAT. Trim Away with a Treat a Day with our Amazing Slimming Plan.' Louise eyed her bosom and thighs with distaste and fled. If only she'd managed to get her figure back after the twins...

*****

'It's me, Louise, Aunt Ethel.' She kissed the old lady lightly on the cheek.

'How good of you to call, Jean dear.'

Sometimes Louise wondered why she bothered visiting the Sunset Home for Gentle Folk when her Great Aunt was so confused. The care assistant brought tea and Aunt Ethel launched into a rambling anecdote.

'…I had nothing to wear for my first ball—a fancy dress affair—and Aunt Flo said she had the very thing in the attics where we kept all the junk. My dear, the place was all over dust, even though the maids spring-cleaned annually. When Aunt Flo found the black tin trunk she was looking for, it was quite clean inside, and there, among layers of tissue paper was the prettiest gown I'd ever seen. "It's for you dear," Aunt Flo beamed.

"Oh I could never take it, it's yours," I protested.

"It always passes from aunt to niece and I'm giving it to you. Great—I don't know how many times great—Aunt Lizzie's wedding gown." Well, you can imagine, I was quite the belle of the ball at Evie Carlisle's Coming Out. I hope you're looking after it dear, it's only in trust till the next generation you know.'

Louise hadn't the heart to disillusion her, but she'd no idea what the old girl was on about. Besides, she didn't have an aunt, let alone a niece. Her mother, Jean, had never mentioned the tradition.

*****

A few weeks later, still evading the Sirens at the Village Hall, she visited her mother.

'I'm thinking of selling up and going into sheltered accommodation. If I put The Old Rectory on the market now I'll be all ready to move into a lodge at Orchard Place when they finish Phase 2. I've already put my name down.' The phone rang. 'That will be the Estate Agent. Hello. Jean Power.'

Louise found herself climbing the narrow attic staircase. Clerical fathers had begotten clerical sons for generations, and The Rectory had stayed in the family until Grandfather John declared himself apostate, made his fortune and bought the Georgian pile when the church sold it off as uneconomic. As a child, Louise had been scared of the shrouded shapes, the scurryings of small rodents, and she'd avoided the attics ever since. A festoon of spiders' webs brushed her face, and an army of motes danced in the shafts of sunlight streaming through the barred windows that crouched beneath the rafters. Louise began sneezing and used her scarf as a mask.

It was eerie, but not threatening. If Mother was moving, muggins here would be responsible for sorting out centuries of debris. Her brother Graham would hardly return from New Zealand. At last, mono-chromed beyond the furthermost splash of sunlight, a pile of rectangular shapes. Why had they banished the cats to below stairs all those years ago? The poor leather suitcases were gnawed to shreds, with little drifts of fabric spilling out. Louise's spirits sank. Recoiling from the uncleanliness, she shunted the cases aside to reveal a trunk that had withstood the ravages of time. As she pulled it into the light, the grey gave way to grimy black metal.

The lid was stuck fast, but eventually responded to the WD40 Louise had sneaked from the boot-hole. A hint of camphor. At least it was mouse proof, perhaps even moth proof. The layers of yellowing tissue paper rustled as she delved, and there it was, unspoilt, an embroidered muslin dress, high waisted, dangerously low cut, with little puffed sleeves. Tentatively, Louise held it up and the classical folds hung as elegantly as they had on Jane Austen's girls. Surely, it couldn't be so old? This thought was vaguely disquieting. She sacrificed her scarf to a beam and tenderly draped the dress on it. Louise trembled with excitement, but the light was fading and her mother was calling her from the garden door far below.

'I've made the tea dear.' Louise found she didn't want to share her find with her mother, who would doubtless monopolize it, or even claim to be the intended recipient herself. A pale shape remained. Paper. Newspaper? She stowed it carefully into her shoulder bag, and replaced the dress until she could smuggle it out on Mother's Bridge Day.

*****

Louise spread out the brittle newspaper on her kitchen table, caught her breath as she made out a date: 1798, an advert for muslin. She googled 'regency costume' and discovered that the end of the eighteenth century had marked a dramatic change in fashion. In fear of the guillotine, the rump of the French aristocrats had discarded their frippery and donned the new English styles that aimed at classical simplicity. It seemed that white, as modelled by marble statues, was the favourite colour. Bubbling with glee, Louise confided her story to her new neighbour, Stella, who taught history at Little Baddenham High School. Stella suggested a costume expert. The costume expert would doubtless expect her to donate the gown to the museum, but it was hers, hers to pass on to her niece, however putative...

*****

When Louise got the gown home, she held her treasure against herself in front of the mirror. It was inches too small, but the figure she saw was that of a radiant young girl.

Then she received an Invitation.

*****

'Welcome to TRIM AND TREAT Louise. You've done the hardest bit, coming through that door.' Louise sat uncomfortably amid the gaggle of ladies, marginally less fat or more gaunt than before. 'And have you got something special to trim for Louise?'

'I want to be able to get into Great—I don't know how many times great—Aunt Lizzie's wedding gown. I should think it's size 8.'

'Your what?'

'You can't wear an antique like that!'

Louise couldn't even rationalise her compulsion to wear the heirloom.

'Why?'

'For a bi-centenary recreation of Jane Austen's Netherfield Ball.'

'Well, that's a bit different. How long have we got?' 'Till the 21st of October.' The class gasped. 'Yes, this year, 2013.'

*****

The girls took to going for a post-weigh-in celebration at The Crown.

'D'you know anything about this Aunt Lizzie, Louise?' asked Stella, who had joined Trim and Treat.

'Not really.'

'You've got a name and a date, why don't you go on Ancestry.co.uk?'

'But I'm much too busy — being a single mum's no joke you know.'

*****

Mentored by the twins and Stella, Louise trawled the records, deciphered the neat printed copperplate, the crabbed handwriting.

> 'Banns of Marriage, 1798…. between Charles Richard Aldous, of this parish, bachelor, and Elizabeth Louisa Power, also of this parish, spinster, were published on the three Sundays underwritten, that is to say on Sunday the 13th of May 1798… by me, John Power, Rector.'

Louise pictured the young bride preparing for the wedding day, trying on the new gown, trimming her bonnet, stealing bashful kisses from her groom in the orchard when her mother wasn't looking.

Marriage Register: the spidery hand, this time in pencil, faded out with a vague squiggle in the middle of the entry. The date had been recorded though, 30th May. Louise felt suspended in anti-climax. She dredged her mind for an explanation. Had he jilted her, or she him? But the couple of her imagination were so happy together, with all their lives before them and a long line of children…

Perhaps the wedding had been postponed. Louise searched feverishly, but to no avail.

Eventually, she tracked down a later entry — Charles had married Catherine Roberts, not his Lizzie. 'Nothing changes,' snorted Louise, 'all men are fickle.' She searched on. Poor little Lizzie had died, aged nineteen, three days after her proposed wedding day. Louise found herself weeping for her dead kinswoman, snatched away in the flower of her youth. She was too distressed to investigate more generations.

Slimming and curiosity about the dress consumed Louise, but she found no clues in the grand pre-sale clear out. She was loathe to ask her mother, and Great Aunt Ethel was seldom rational.

*****

On a soft autumn day, Louise gave a final quick check of the ancestral home before relinquishing the keys to the estate agent. The orchard was strewn with a few desultory apples and scatterings of yellow leaves. No more Powers would play there, watched over by stay-at-home maiden Aunts. The Old Rectory, somnolent and musty inside, awaited the architect's concepts. Louise wandered from empty room to empty room, glimpsing snatches of her childhood. She opened her old bedroom door, and there was Lizzie, tossing and turning on her sick bed, with white cap and flushed face. Beside her knelt a young girl, bathing her fore-head with a damp cloth. It must be her niece. The name Isabella came to mind. Isabella was all but husband high.

'Bella,' came the hoarse voice, struggling to speak, 'You must have my wedding gown when I am gone.'

'Don't say that Lizzie, I heard the apothecary tell your mama that the fever would soon abate.'

'I think not. I insist that you have my gown as a remembrance of me, for you and I spent such happy hours working upon it.'

'Oh Lizzie, you are so good.' The head sank back into the pillows. 'I will call your Mama now.' A slight draught of skirts, and the picture faded.

*****

Louise pulled the front door shut and pocketed the key. School-run day, but she'd just have time for the churchyard. Lizzie's grave nestled in a shower of rosehips. Misty eyed, she searched the family plot for Isabella: Isabella Elizabeth, the right age, a happy matron.

*****

Louise did manage to squeeze herself into the gown for the Netherfield Ball, where her hand for the first country dance was requested, if not by Mr Darcy, by Mr Right.

She never returned to TRIM AND TREAT. Whenever she feels tempted to gorge herself, she admires the muslined figure posed in the glass cabinet her new man has made.

Graham's last Skype announced a wedding and a coming baby.

Louise fervently prays for a nephew.

Time and Time Again

Tucked away in the corner of the cottage, Dickon lay a-snug under his blanket, breathing in the sweet smell of straw. Dong, dong, dong, dong, dong struck the church clock. Those outlandish folk would not be a-troubling him yet awhile.

*****

It was strange how sometimes they were there, sometimes not. But the oddest thing was how the cottage had reappeared like a mushroom in the night.Ced had been so sure that it was gone for ever, but there it was, every beam, nook, and cranny familiar. Was it witchcraft?

They burned witches…

His family had all lived there before plague had struck, he was quite certain of that. Then, one day, word had come that scores of people hard by in the village of Melford were dead.

'Tis time to flit, for all Sir William's orders that none should leave the manor,' his father had said, brushing little swirls of wool from his doublet. No-one from the Hall had sickened yet.

The family travelled long days and nights with their bundles, then his mother sneezed, and sneezed again, then came the fearful red botches that no physic could cure. One by one, they did die, his mother, his father, and his two little sisters. Too puny to dig, lashed by rain, Dickon heaved the corpses into a heathland pit and covered them tenderly with bracken as the sky grew dark. A sudden warm stillness, then burst after burst of thunder cracked through the air, great sheets of light blazed over the bushes and trees, then as quickly subsided into little dancing flashes in the desolate landscape. There being no priest, Dickon muttered some prayers, hoping God would hear above the deafening noise. With the dawn, Dickon set off, wandering on alone, begging food, eating berries, trapping conies, sleeping under hedges, in hay ricks, in barns, longing only to join his family in heaven.

*****

After the plague had passed and more moons than he could tell, Dickon had come upon Melford once more.

Near the church he heard running footsteps, a young girl seeking the priest. Dickon ducked behind a headstone.

'Father, come quickly, my Grandam has fallen in a fit and is near dead.'

'Pray God it be not too late, my child, for if she dies unshriven she shall surely suffer the pains of Purgatory until the Last Day.' Fear clutched coldly at Dickon's heart. No priest had absolved his family... Could it be that they were not in heaven? He crossed himself, kneeled to pray for their souls though he knew not the words.

Fearful of the Steward's wrath, he crept over the fields hard by the Hall, but no kith and kin could he find. Had Sir William ordered his father's cottage to be carted away as punishment for flitting without leave?

Desolate, Dickon roamed on.

*****

Next midsummer, Melford drew him like a lodestone. The gossips were washing linen in the river.

'Aye, Master Clifford, he that was the Steward at Kentwell, died a good death.'

'God rest his soul!'

Dickon stopped in his tracks. Sir William would surely appoint a new Steward who would doubtless hold no grudge. He would seek him out and ask for work...

Dickon plodded up the long avenue, his heart pounding, the hard road biting into his bare feet, black, evil-smelling. Beyond the gates, the Hall basked in the sun and through the trees he could see his own cottage. He blinked, unable to believe his eyes. Mazed, he hovered at the open door, greeted by the comforting smell of seething roots and wood smoke.

'Why, welcome cousin. I did not look for thee till the morrow, but do thou come in. What is thy name?'

'Dickon, mistress.' The woman was a stranger.

'Do thou call me Cousin Rose. Mack, my good man, will be here e'er long.' How oddly Cousin Rose spoke. He eyed the pottage, the smell feeding the emptiness in his belly.

'Why, hast thou not breakfasted child?' He stared, not understanding.

'Well, just a sup before the punters come.'

*****

And that was how he came to have food for his belly and a good dry bed. After the pottage, he had felt the heaviness of sleep upon him, felt Cousin Rose's kind arms take him to the snug little bed hidden by a curtain.

That first night, he slept long, and awoke to the clamour of excited young voices. If he kept his eyes fast shut, they would think he yet slept. But he needed to piss… He crossed himself under the blanket, peeked out round the curtain and opened one eye. It must be witchcraft… A dozen, nay a score, of monstrous children, garbed outlandishly, were shouting, laughing, pointing, staring, most unmannerly.

'What's he doing lying there?'

Cousin Rose put her cool hand on his forehead. 'What ails thee child? God forfend thou hast an ague. Do thou keep thy bed, and I shall prepare a concoction of goodly herbs to abate thy fever.' Dickon was bursting, pushed off the blanket, sneaked outside and pissed behind the woodpile.

'Ague,' she'd said. What was that? He'd heard of 'agyoo.' She couldn't mean the plague could she? He crept back into the bed, Cousin Rose's face blurred down at him. He felt hot all over. His mother had had a raging fever, and she was dead... He shut his eyes, blocking out the stares, the grinning faces. Then the sound of the intruders drifted away.

'Are you OK Dickon? If you've got a temperature, I'll give you some Junior Aspro before the next lot of punters come. Perhaps you'd better go back to the campsite. What station's your mother on? '

'My mother is dead of the plague these three years since,' he said weakly, his mind swimming. 'My mother is in heaven. And my father, and my little sisters...' But were they? If only he could be sure... Noises without made him hide his head. He spat out the bitter white thing she'd thrust into his mouth. Rose tugged at the blanket.

'Nay, in verray truth Dickon, where is thy mother?'

'My mother is in heaven...' He crossed himself, praying it was true.

*****

As the days passed, Dickon grew bolder, left his bed, but there was much he did not understand. He dwelt in the cottage working with his cousins, but they did not lie there — they came each morning as the church clock struck nine, worked at their housekeeping, and vanished strangely after the company had gone. Then Dickon would hide behind the woodpile before taking sole possession of his old home. He never thought to follow them, but stoked the ailing fire, put roots in the pot to seethe, then went out to set his traps.

Each day, there was much company, more even than at Bury Fair. Many wore spectacles, strangely supported about the ears, and Dickon marvelled at how learned they must be for all they asked the silliest questions.

'What are you doing?' They would say, though t'was the simplest task he was about.

'Do thou tell the young master what thou doest, Dickon,' Cousin Rose would say.

'I be carding the wool… washing the roots for the pottage… binding osiers to sweep the floor… skinning the cony for the pot…'

'Heaven forfend, 'tis no fit task for one so young,' she'd said the first time he'd brought back a cony, still warm. How strange!

'Where do you live?' they asked.

'I dwell here.'

'No, in real life.' What did they mean?

'Where do your Mum and Dad live?' They were asking about his mother and father it seemed.

'They did die of the plague… '

One day, his thoughts were drowned by a mighty roaring, nearer and nearer that filled the whole sky, more fearful even than the thunder he'd heard on the heath after burying his family. Sobbing, he fled to his bed, hid trembling under the blanket.

'What's that then?' A boy's cruel fingers poked at him, then Cousin Rose's calm voice.

'Nay young master, I do see nothing flying through the air, 'tis but a fantasy of thine own imagining.' Peace was restored, but not for Dickon. After the company had left, his heart a flutter, he crept up to Cousin Mack and plucked his sleeve.

'Are we in purgatory coz? Shall I ever see my mother and father and little sisters?'

'What meanest thou?'

'I fear they cannot be in heaven, for there was no priest to shrive them, and I did bury them in the heath...' Tears of guilt poured down his cheeks.

'You don't believe all that rubbish?' There's no such place.'

Dickon was astounded. They burned heretics...

'But...'

Cousin Rose was raking out the fire. 'It's OK Dickon, if they were good people, your family is in heaven with God.'

Could this be true?

'Off you go then and find Mummy. You're the best kid we've ever had. See you next year! Bye.'

*****

Rosie Cruickshank and Ian Mackay plodded to the Undercroft to grab a cup of coffee before going to the campsite to pack.

'The last day! It's supposed to be a holiday, for heaven's sake, but I've never worked so hard in my life.' Rosie pulled off her coif, letting her hair fall loose.

'Still, I suppose we're willing to be exploited to fill His Lordship's coffers.'

'Come off it, Ian, we're doing it because we enjoy it — and he needs the money to keep up the house. Kentwell wouldn't survive without the Event.'

'D'you remember the first year we came as punters? The Living History thing was totally mind-blowing,' said Ian.

'And now we're part of it! All that costume making, all the research into peasant life — it's worth every jot of blood sweat and tears. I thought I'd seen it all in Third World countries, but this is something else...'

'It feels like 24 7. Those re-enactors who turn up for a spot of jolly Bank Holiday jousting at Little Baddenham Castle don't know they're born.' Ian drained his plastic cup. 'I'm glad I didn't opt for the pottery — too much like the day job!'

'There was another plane today. Young Dickon had *me* scared witless too!' added Rosie.

'You'd think he'd been born to it.'

'Come to think, Ian, I've never seen him at breakfast or dinner. I wonder where he goes.'

'Perhaps they're in B and B in Long Melford.'

'Could be local.'

Master Warrener creaked down beside them, quaffed his tea and belched.

'Haven't you been doing us proud then? Fresh rabbit every day!' grinned Rosie.

'Not me Mistress!' The Warrener leered knowingly, fingering his ferrets in his hose. A group of gentry drooped in, sweating and swollen-footed from their heavy costumes.

'If they play 'Greensleeves' on their plastic recorders one more time, or tell me about computers and mobile phones, I'll beat the brats roundly about the ears.' Lady Waldegrave collapsed onto a bench and kicked off her shoes.

'Tis hands-on experience they need,' guffawed the Warrener.

'But explaining a modern concept in terms a Tudor peasant could understand well exerciseth the mind,' expounded the Schoolmaster.

'And some of the little ones believe we're real,' added Rosie, 'so we have to play up to them.'

His Lordship's administrative assistant breezed in. 'Hi everyone.'

'Fiona, who does our young Dickon belong to? He's so into his role he won't tell us a thing. Just comes out with the stock retort about his parents being dead of the plague, only he's worried his mother might not be in heaven after all!'

'Dickon? Who's he?'

'The boy you promised us.'

'But the Shepherds didn't turn up.'

'What? Then who on earth is this Dickon? He appeared on the first day — a bit shell shocked — though he soon got into the way of it. He's fantastic.'

Fiona's latest swain swept her off.

*****

Dickon woke to more chimes than he could tell on his two hands. The Angelus? But nobody had come. No voices; no cheerful sounds from the smithy, nor the woodcutters; no friendly wood smoke, nor seething roots; no distant harmony of maidens singing: 'Rose, Rose, Rose, shall I ever see thee wed?' Silence, but for the shriek of the peacocks, the twittering of birds, then that other sound, a thunderous roaring from the sky, mightier than a dozen bulls. He fled into the cottage, into his bed, under his blanket and hid, trembling, sobbing, pressing his hands over his ears.

When he woke, the sun was well down in the sky, duck-egg streaked with sanguine and peach. He gazed out at the Hall, shining with the light of a thousand stars, great sheets of light blazing from the windows over the courtyard, but not a soul in sight. Had the people been but spirits?

They burnt witches…

Or had the roaring thing struck down those outlandish people with the plague? Or had the fiery chariot taken them up into heaven in a whirlwind like the prophet Elijah?

The mist in Dickon's head swirled around, then cleared. Perhaps the chariot had taken his family up into heaven, there had been noise enough and fire… At last he understood. His father, his mother, his little sisters were indeed among the saved, and meanwhile he had shelter, wood for the fire, food for his belly, and a good dry bed.

Purists will find that plague did not strike Long Melford between the Black Death (1348–1350) and 1604, by which time protestant theology had overturned the concept of purgatory. However, the threat of plague was ever present, and there were outbreaks in England in 1535 and 1543. Henry VIII, though Head of the Church of England, largely retained Roman Catholic doctrine. But then this Tall Tale is fiction, and Long Melford is not quite Long Melford.

THE OTHER SIDE

Jane and Hannah had been inseparable at school but they'd somehow lost touch, bar a sterile exchange of season's greetings, until they met up at a big Five O lunch in their home town, Little Baddenham. 'I'm still in the same house,' Hannah said over the canapés, 'although Steve and I split up after the kids left home. Why don't you stay over so we can catch up, Jane?'

Thirty odd years ago, Hannah and Steve had taken Jane, as chief bridesmaid elect, to inspect the house before they exchanged contracts. Jane vaguely remembered a rosebay-willow-herb infested gap where Number 13 should have been, the wraiths of chimney breasts in the brickwork of the exposed gable end. The Edwardian semis had front gardens barely big enough to swing a cat.

'Bombed out towards the end of the Second World War and not rebuilt because of some feud between the heirs,' the estate agent had brayed. 'The site's remained a bone of contention for years. That's why I was able to negotiate a rock bottom price!'

Their third Christmas letter complained that builders next door were out-vying the new baby on the noise front. Now, as the friends parked in convoy, Number 13, all plate glass and garage, looked totally incongruous in the winter gloom.

Jane recalled Hannah's teenage bedroom as the prototype for today's murky dens. Number 15 wasn't exactly dirty, but she was disturbed by the all-pervasive clutter: carpets highlighted by tatters of tissue; sheets of paper that had missed the bin; the disorderly pile of crockery queuing up for the dish washer.

'I suppose Steve traded me in for a tidier model because of my mess, Jane,' Hannah said ruefully over the stir-fry. 'I just can't get on top of things.' Hannah's eyes were twitching disconcertingly.

*****

On that January night, they sprawled in front of the gas fire in the wide upstairs sitting room, sipping Jane's gift of red wine, burning joss-sticks, playing Simon and Garfunkel, talking endlessly to recapture the lost years. The big mottled mirror over the chimney breast all but reflected their younger selves amid the flicker of candles. But as the evening wore on, Jane couldn't help noticing Hannah's glance straying furtively towards the book-lined alcove on the right of the fireplace.

'What's wrong?' Hannah jerked her features back into a smile. 'It's nothing,' and another drink later, 'if I tell you, Jane, you'll never believe it.'

'Try me!

The old Hannah had been overflowing with vivacity. Like many of Jane's clients, lethargy hung heavily on her gaunt frame.

'The whole thing's bizarre! I've been lacking in get-up-and-go since I've been on my own. No, don't ask after my writing. The muse is dead, caput. My doctor calls it depression but, believe it or not, I actually enjoy my own company and not being behoven to anyone.

'It all began last June. I nodded off over some escapist thing on TV. You know how you feel disorientated when you come to? When I managed to open my eyes, something wasn't quite right. The alcove. No book shelves there, just a solid door. Some force pulled me to my feet, shunted me across the room, connected my hand to the brass door-handle, turned it. A wide shaft of light, broken by my shadow, pierced the darkened room. An opposite door, still in motion, was silhouetted by brightness beyond.'

Classic closed door syndrome, thought Jane.

'That first time,' continued Hannah, 'it was like looking into a roped-off room in a National Trust property. What little I could see seemed strangely familiar, even the grandfather clock. I could visualize the flights of stairs beyond, the turned bannisters... But Number 13 wasn't Edwardian, it was nineteen seventies...

'I was desperate to explore, but the invisible barrier buffeted me back. Then the two grandfather clocks growled themselves up to strike midnight. In unison. I glanced back into my room to check out my clock, turned towards its twin, only to find my bookshelves had reconstituted themselves.'

The joss sticks smouldered, the gas coals sputtered, the wine glowed ruby red. Hannah's black cat, Midnight, stalked in, rubbed itself against her legs, purring loudly, before shredding the Kleenex newly dropped from her sleeve.

'You must have been dreaming,' Jane urged. 'I have a recurring dream about discovering hitherto unknown rooms, generally spider-ridden attics or cellars, ripe for renovation. The shrinks say it's about trying to access unfulfilled ideals and ambitions.' *Best not let on to Hannah that she was now a therapist. It wasn't ethical to counsel your friends.*

'Maybe, but I *wasn't* asleep Jane!' Hannah protested. Her eyes had developed a nervous tick. 'It was like being in *Alice through the Looking Glass*. Spooky or what! I was frantic to discover what lay beyond that door. Night after night I recreated the ambience, but nothing happened. I couldn't settle to anything, prowled around like a caged panther. I moved the furniture, I bought that hideaway office-in-a-cupboard for my computer, so I could shut away the clutter of barely-started novels and stories. I would sit there admiring the unit's sleek lines and its promise of literary success instead of getting down to writing.

'Then one day, as Grandfather struck noon, that door materialized. Through it, I could see a trim woman with sleek dark hair totally absorbed in clattering away at an ancient sit-up-and-beg typewriter. Her bureau sported nothing more than a pen, pencils, an exercise book and a neat sheaf of typescript. Full stop. I could just make out family photos, a man in uniform, a couple of children. I watched till she finished, sighed contentedly, and left the room. I hurtled through that door, spun round. Yes, the fireplace was identical to mine. The pictures were such as I'd conjured up in my mind's eye... I stepped forward and the bookshelves slammed shut.

'Panic wasn't in it! I scurried across the room, peeked onto the landing... Footsteps... Perhaps I was stuck in a time warp. I opened my mouth but no scream came out...

'Then the shelves opened like a book and I was home and dry, shaking, cowering on the floor.'

'Poor you.' They were getting maudlin by now.

'Are you quite sure you weren't dreaming?' *The old Hannah had never shown any signs of psychosis.* 'You mentioned the clock? Did you notice the time when you got back from the other side?'

'I was in real Greenwich Time, honestly. I went outdoors and checked that Number 13 was as brazenly seventies as ever. I mowed the lawn, pulled up a few weeds, and heard the one o'clock pips as I went in to get lunch.'

'That sounds convincing! How was the woman dressed?'

'I can't say I noticed, nothing extraordinary, but I don't believe in ghosts Jane. No way! I grew bolder since apparently I was invisible, except to her cat, who ignored me, as felines do. Even the moggy was familiar, as black and as green-eyed as my Midnight.

'Another time, there was a sparkling new Remington. You'd expect a pair of semis to mirror each other architecturally, but it was more than that, Jane. The furnishings, the décor, the artefacts, all seemed familiar, every detail like something I'd ogled in *Country Life*. I'd always longed to be the perfect home-maker, the ideal mother, Jane, surrounded by harmony and beautiful things, to be a creative genius. But I'd never achieved these aspirations, just muddled along.'

Classic low self-esteem, thought Jane.

'The reverse book shelves were usually hidden by the open door, but one day the contents were visible and I discovered a select row of novels, signed, "Anna". Where had I seen those titles before? In my dreams of course. Do you think I'm schizophrenic Jane? Or have I got a brain tumour that alters my perceptions?' Her shoulder twitched, her fingers circled the top of her glass till it shrieked.

'I don't think you should worry about mental illness, Hannah. I don't entirely discount the paranormal. Some people believe in a parallel universe. I think you've stumbled into a ghost house. It must be all of fifty years since the bomb, perhaps it's having a reshuffle.'

'Perhaps… But there's more. I was looking out of her bedroom window one day—unlike mine, her garden was oozing with vegetables. I froze behind the curtain as she rushed in, rapidly untying a parcel. For the first time I saw her face. It was my face, a better tended face, wrinkle-free, with not a grey hair in sight, but incontrovertibly my own face. Surely she must have heard my gasp? But no, she was trying on the new dress, pirouetting in front of the triple cheval mirror. The cat was unimpressed, but catching sight of its own reflection, catapulted round the mirror to tackle its rival. I crept up behind her, and there we were, side by side, as like as two cherries on a stem. A twin adopted at birth? A doppelganger? An alter ego? Was one of us dead, a ghost? And if so, which? When the whirling of the room subsided, there was just one image in the central mirror.

' "Who are you?" I gasped. The next thing I remember is waking up stiff and cold on my own sofa. The door hasn't appeared since.'

'Wow!' Jane murmured, and suggested Horlicks and bed. Poor Hannah looked totally drained. The candles and joss sticks had long ago burnt out. Hannah's cat lay unperturbed before the ever glowing fire.

*****

In the morning, after a night wrestling with Hannah's story and how best to help her, Jane restored order to the kitchen. By the time her friend came down, draggled from sleep, Jane was Googling the East Anglian Daily Times' archive with a pot of strong coffee beside her.

'I don't suppose you can remember the date of your first encounter?'

'Last June, it was a Friday. Yes, Friday the thirteenth. But I'm not superstitious…'

'OK. Look at this.' A headline: *Bomb Blast Strikes Little Baddenham on Friday the 13th!*' and a muzzy picture of the debris dated June 1941.

'Oh my God!'

'Fifty years exactly.'

Jane scrolled down. An eminent lady novelist had been found dead in the rubble. Her Remington, un‑damaged, had been taken to the Home Guard HQ.

'Weird or what!'

'D'you know, I think I've seen that self-same typewriter in the town museum.'

'Then let's go and see, not that it would prove anything, there must have been loads of them made.'

*****

The museum was cold, less so under the spotlights. Hannah strode towards the retro Remington, black, cumbersome.

'Aah!' A gasp of recognition. She stretched out her hand, fingered the keys and smiled beatifically.

'I can feel a stream of words pouring out from that keyboard, Jane. Her words? My Words? I can't wait to get them down.'

Gone was the nervous tick, gone was the apathy.

*****

Before Jane set off home, they indulged in lunch and mulled wine in front of a roaring fire at The Crown.

'That stuff in the East Anglian is hardly a rational explanation,' said the new Hannah.

'So what! But the mirror house personified the antithesis of your own failures. Now you're in touch with your better self, you can move on.'

'I suppose…' Hannah took a big gulp of the hot punch, her eyes gleaming. 'And I've got a subject for a new novel!' They clinked glasses.

'*Carpe Diem*. Get writing girl!'

OFF OF THE SHELF

I didn't start looking round till after I get my Degree Absolute. Well, my face look more like a road map than a spring chicken, but what d'you expect after three husbands? Mind you, Mirabel, unlike them, I never went in for no hanky-panky till I were a Free Woman. Yes, the Burnt Vanilla today. There's nothing like a cut and blow-dry to boost your morals.

I likes to have a bit of a gossip when I'm stacking shelves—you don't get much feed-back from baked beans, leastways not when they're still in their tins. Most of the girls are younger than me, with kiddies and hubbies at home, or not as the case may be. Things was different when Dave left me with three under-fives, the bastard. I could of coped with his boozing and blooming tempers till he went off on the lorries and that bitch Gloria got her claws into him. And the chaps at work are all under forty except the Manager and his wife's going to be a lady vicar. Didn't stop Dawn French having it off with

Mike Barrett from *Casualty* though. Then Cliff, he turn up. He'd been off sick with some gentleman's trouble when I first start work at Alldays Super Store. He were pushing the Produce trolley, piled high with boxes of bananas and carrots, and cucumbers and courgettes. Now Tinned Veg is about as far away as you can get from Produce, but I could tell Cliff were a fine upstanding chap and more my age. I could just picture us dancing together at the Christmas Do, so I took to reverting my crate past Produce whenever I could. Cliff, he's got rugged good looks, bit balding but a lovely smile and such a twinkle in them deep blue eyes. He got that blond hair you can't tell if it's going white or not.

'Hallo Marilyn,' he'd say. How are you gal?' Lovely smile Cliff's got, and I like the way he handle the fruit, checking out each apple and pear as he put them on the shelf. And I'd say, 'Hello Cliff. Busy day we're having.'

This weren't getting me very far, till I overhear the Manager say they'd have to get someone to take over Teas and Coffees. Now the Tea and Coffee aisle's right next to Produce, so I say how I'd like a change. So they swap me over so I could talk my heart out to Cliff whenever I like. Sometimes his son Andy he come in, and I could see what a fine figure of a man Cliff must of bin when he were young, talk about sexy. You should see them in their black leathers, Mirabel!

Cliff, he got this big Harley Davison, all chrome and black, and he tell me how on his day off he ride all round Suffolk, even up Norwich, for the sheer joy of it. 'With the wind in your face and the open road, there's nothing like it,' he say. 'Sometimes I rides her for miles and miles and I revs her up and I revs her up. Takes your mind off of things. Accelerating,' he say, 'sheer acceleration!' Mind you, Mirabel, I don't fancy riding pillion on that great monster.

He tell me he been divorced twice. He's a bit bottled up Cliff, and it all come out in dribs and drabs. Andy's mum buggered off to Canada with their little girl, leaving him to bring up Andy.

'She shouldn't of treated you like that,' I say, 'the bitch.' When that bastard Dave left me, it were a real struggle bringing up three kiddies on the social and I didn't want to be took for an Unmarried Mother. You chaps are lucky, your ring finger don't tell the whole world your marriageable status.'

'Best thing ever happen to me,' he say. I were gobsmacked. If that sod Dave had made away with our Diane, I'd have got my teeth into him where that hurt, I can tell you.

'I should never of married her,' he say, 'only she didn't take no precautions, the stupid git, and she fell for Tracey. I had to stand by her, but it's my firm belief she done it to trap me into marrying her.' Cliff was checking the bananas for splits in their skins. 'I never really loved her, not like I loved Sally, she was the love of my life.'

That bring a tear to my eye. 'Oh Cliff,' I say, putting my hand on his arm. 'That were ever so good of you. And then she went and treated you like dirt, the bitch.'

My heart raced. If he'd never loved his last, perhaps he might start fancying me. When he'd gone, I go over to Health and Beauty and get some

Clairol what say it cover grey, and it weren't even On Offer.

'Andy, he's left home,' he say one day, tipping out a box of onions. 'He's got hisself a job and moved in with his girlfriend.'

'Int that lovely,' I say feeling all weak about the knees. 'That's ever so romantic.'

Over the weeks, Cliff, he got quite broody, complained about the long winter evenings with no one to talk to.

'You can always come up mine,' I offered. 'I'll make you a nice Toad in the Hole.' My new colour really suit me, all the girls said so, but Cliff, he never noticed.

Then one day it all come pouring out. He had nothing to live for. He were that repressed. If only he hadn't split up with Sally all those years ago.

'We was too young,' he say. 'We started arguing, about me going off with the boys for a spin on the bikes, about her spending too much on fancy clothes, and we didn't know how to sort it out. Irreversible Break Down it say in the divorce papers. There was never any of that magic with Andy's mum,' sighed Cliff. 'I can't stop thinking about Sally. I still love her to bits after half a lifetime!'

Full marks for loyalty points. I was gutted. But you never know. He took out a photo from his inside pocket, next his heart it were. Sally, she were ever so pretty, with a smile to make your heart stop.

'What happen to her?' I say.

'God knows. The last thing I heard she were immigrating to Canada with some bloke.'

'Poor Cliff! I lost the Love of my Life too. None of them others ever measured up to my Dave. We was only seventeen when we met and it were Love at First Sight. We was happy as the day is long, and that's not to mention the nights, till that bitch stole him away.'

If me and Cliff hadn't been on the shop floor, I'd of given him a big hug. As sure as eggs is eggs. You want me to get under the drier now Mirabel?

Anyways, when I come back from the Costa del Sol, I got moved to Tinned Fruit so I didn't see so much of Cliff. After all them relegations, perhaps he were avoiding me.

Then one day Cliff, he come looking for me. His face were all aglow, one big grapefruit segment ear to ear.

'She ring me up from Canada. Sally ring me up.' You could of knocked me down with a feather.
'That must of cost her,' I say to hide my agony. 'And?'

'It were just like it used to be, all the old magic. Like rewinding my life. She's got a family out there, but her bloke died, and she couldn't stop thinking about me and how it might of been. I'm going out to see her just as soon as I can.'

'But Cliff,' I urged, seizing his arm and gazing deep into his eyes, 'you can't never go back — it can't never be the same. Just keep hold of your memories safe and sound or it'll all get spoilt.' But he just beamed back.

'Not this. That's Meant, the way it happened. I know that's Meant. I were out on the bike after work last Thursday, just driving around aimless like, and I come to this T junction. I stops, and wonder which way will I go. And I felt this urge to turn right, and I go down this narrow old winding lane, and blast, don't I come out right next her old house. So I turn off the engine, and I'm sat there, just thinking and thinking of her, and it's like there's these waves of her coming through the air. And it's like I'm up there in the sky looking down on us together, only I can't quite tell if it's us then or us now.'

'Oh Cliff,' I say, 'that's ever so romantic.'

'And then last night, she ring me up. She say she couldn't stop thinking about me. She have the same blooming sense of waves coming and going through the ether at dinner time on Thursday. So she move heaven and earth to get my number and there she were.'

'It's just like one of them old films,' I say, so he couldn't tell I was crying because I'd lost him for ever. Well, that took Cliff months and months to save up to go out to Canada, what with all the phone bills and the minimum wage and his holiday entitlement. And I start wondering how she get his phone number. Just before he set off on his great adventure, I ask him.

'You can find out anything on the internet,' he say.

Well, I'm not exactly computer illiterate, but my Diane's kids tap away at them games and websites. So, I say to our Callum one day, 'I want you to look up your grandad Dave. Don't let on to your Mum, that's a secret.'

Cliff's back from Canada tomorrow. That's why I'm having my hair done. Let me see. Oh, that's ever so nice. Them highlights take years off of me. You done a lovely job Mirabel. The minute I see his face, I'll know what the score is. And if he's all down in the mouth, I'll be there for him with wide open arms to console him and you never know. But if he's all over smiles, then I'll get on to Dave.

Keep the change, Mirabel.

Grandfather Strikes Again

St Edmund's Church clock struck four as Stella plonked her briefcase heavily on her doorstep and fumbled for her front-door key.

'All right Georgie, good boy.' Georgie was frantically beating the door with his tail amid frenzied yelps of anticipation. Once over the threshold, she fended off his wet embrace. Out of the corner of her eye, she noticed a tell-tale scrap of white paper. 'Georgie. You didn't, bad dog.' Georgie, having come fifth-hand from the dogs' home, was a tad unpredictable. Not only did he emulate the Andrex puppy, but he had been known to catch the post. However, his bed revealed no shreds of envelope.

Stella couldn't understand why Jonny hadn't contacted her. They'd been an item, hadn't they, before she'd moved to Little Baddenham for the beginning of the spring term? His voice-mail continued to give the same formal message. She emailed, she texted, she made every excuse in the book for him. She confided in her new friend Louise from TRIM AND TREAT, the slimming club she'd joined, to make herself more attractive to Jonny, who was the athletic type.

'If you try too hard, you'll only put him off,' advised Louise, who had suffered a broken marriage.

Why, oh why, had she left Worcester at such a delicate stage in their relationship? But she hadn't even met Jonny when she accepted the post. She'd been hankering to return to East Anglia and, when a job came up at Little Baddenham High School, she'd leapt at the chance. She was charmed by the pretty village. Correction: town. The locals bridled alarmingly when visitors and incomers got it wrong. As a historian, Stella had to agree that the 1285 charter granting market status undeniably made it a town, though its size and ambience was more like a village.

She let Georgie out, quickly recalling him from the wintry garden. With the spaniel close at her heels, she took a cup of tea through to the living room. Her heir-loom grandfather clock cleared its throat and ponderously chimed. Four, five, six, she counted.

'You've got it wrong again, you nerd. I'd have thought you would have settled down by now.' Grandfather, like the dog, was unpredictable. His gleaming brass face gazed back blankly. 'Bell of Norwich,' was all it said.

Walking the dog later in the pouring rain, Stella reviewed her day. She'd told the kids about the legend that birds choose their mates upon St Valentine's Day. She'd even read them a bit of Chaucer's *Parliament of Fowls,* natural history, poetry and linguistics all rolled into one.

'Did you get a Valentine, Miss?' they clamoured. And she hadn't, if you didn't count Billy Diggins' anonymous effort. She'd been so sure Jonny would contact her today of all days. She'd made a pact with herself, even told Louise about it: if St Valentine's Day came and went and Jonny still hadn't been in touch, she'd delete him from her phone and put the whole episode behind her as nothing more than a lovely memory. It would be a wrench, she'd been so certain they had something special.

Her eyes watered as she relived their first meeting. They'd both been attending a performance of *The Tempest* at Stratford, and in the interval they'd changed eyes picking up their pre-ordered drinks and sought each other out at the end.

Louise warned Stella of the dangers of a long-distance relationship. 'I married Tom too soon after a weekends only romance, and it all ended in disaster.'

'But you've got the twins.' Louise's twins were in Stella's class. 'And the A14 route takes no time at all.'

After supper, ears alert for the phone, Stella started on a pile of marking. At eight o'clock precisely, Grandfather growled long and ferociously, but failed to chime. Georgie, hackles raised, fur standing on end, snarled to see him off. 'Can't you get anything right?' she accused Grandfather as she pulled down the weight.

When bedtime came, she checked her emails and phone yet again and resigned herself to the inevitable. It was over. She must learn to accept that her relationship with Jonny was a might-have-been, a thing of the past. Georgie snuggled up to her in bed as they listened to *Late Junction*. As the Midnight News came on, Grandfather decided to chime again. Stella counted his muffled tones: one, two, three, four, five, six.

Then silence.

Desolation overcame her.

Then the phone rang distantly. The cradle beside her bed was empty. Georgie sometimes caught the phone. Perhaps he had knocked off the handset. She rushed downstairs, preceded by four short legs. 'No Georgie, don't you dare.'

'Hello,' she said tentatively.

'Is that you Stella? It's me, Jonny. Happy Valentine! It is still Valentine's Day isn't it? I'm suffering from jetlag.'

An upsurge of relief struck her silent: she sat down to catch her breath.

'And before you ask, I've been away on business for five weeks. Top secret. My phone was stolen at the airport and the venue was so remote, the internet was down for my entire stay. When can I come over? We've got a lot of catching up to do!'

Eventually she put the phone down in a fever of happiness. Sensing her mood, Georgie gambolled around her feet. Not to be outdone, Grandfather cleared his throat and thunderously chimed … ten, eleven, twelve, she counted. 'Late again!

His face impassive, Grandfather gathered himself for a final effort, and donged yet one more chime.

THE CRUICKSHANK CHRONICLES IV
THE THREAD OF LIFE

Something woke Laura, but she wasn't ready to open her eyes. Best wait till her thudding pulse calmed down. Besides, she was desperate to finish the dream. She was in some fairground sort of place, not quite the Gala, wailing because she hadn't won a goldfish in a jam-jar… Laura couldn't quite tell where the dream stopped and recollection took over. It wasn't fair, her little sister Joan had already won a goldfish and her brother Henry had won two coconuts. 'Never mind, chickadee,' said her father, 'it would only die.' He was pulling them along like the red Queen in *Alice Through the Looking Glass*. Water was slurping out of the jam-jar. A big blob of Joan's pink candyfloss dropped into it and Joan's face crumpled into a wail. They were getting nowhere fast.

Then they were outside a tent with wavy curtains and a strange spicy smell. A tall man with a black beard and big gold rings in his ears was standing outside. 'Come and have your fortune told by Gypsy Esmerelda,' he was bawling, 'only a penny.' Laura wondered why Father had brought them there. She tugged his sleeve.

'You promised we could go on the Merry-go-round.'

'Later, chickadee.' That was a funny word. There was a picture of a silvery ball like a goldfish bowl and a big hand with squiggly lines drawn on it. Henry had sloped of as usual, but Father stood stock still, fingers on lips. 'Shh,' he said, craning his head towards the curtain with his hand cupped behind his ear. They could just hear whispering voices. Laura found a little gap in the curtain and peeked through. Mother was sitting at a table shrouded in a cloth with funny squiggles on it. Gypsy Esmerelda was gazing at Mother's open hand, fingering it.

'Ah,' she said, 'I see you have a fine man, a fine son, and two little girls.' Her voice sounded funny, foreign.

Joan finished her candyfloss, looked round to check Father wasn't looking and dropped the stick on the ground with a little skip.

'Yes,' breathed Mother, 'I do indeed. 'But what else do you see?' The gypsy let out a long sad 'Ahh...'

'Tell me,' said Mother in her 'you'd better do as you're told' voice.

'I see your lifeline, its thread is cut short.' Mother shrieked and dashed out of the tent. She sent poor Joan and her goldfish flying as she rushed into Father's arms. The gold fish flapped around a bit on the grass then went still. Serve Joan right, but she was bawling now. Neither of her parents took the slightest notice.

'There, there, dear,' Father was saying, 'you know it's all stuff and nonsense.'

'No it's not. Esmerelda truly has the gift of second sight.'

'Rubbish. Everyone knows all about our family…' but Mother couldn't stop sobbing.

Mothers shouldn't cry. It wasn't right.

*****

For Laura, the dream scenario was all too familiar. Every time she had it, the dream broke off at that point. How she yearned to find out what happened next, to find the longed for happy ending where her mother had not mysteriously died just before Laura's tenth birthday. And what on earth had they been doing in a fairground anyway? In those days, her parents would have considered it far too plebeian for the Orchard Place family.

Ah well, she thought, stirring, best wake up now. Something didn't feel right. Geoff should be there… but Geoff had died. Why wasn't the cat snuggling into the small of her back? Momentarily, she was somewhere up in the ceiling, looking down at the white bed. Was it her mother lying there? When she at last opened her eyes, confusion enveloped her. She stretched out for the light switch, but it wasn't there. The window was in the wrong place, a dim figure was gliding across an enormous room. Laura scrabbled for her glasses. Then she remembered, she was in Heath Road Hospital.

They'd trundled her down endless corridors, helped her into this bed at 5 am. Before that, she'd been for hours in a limbo of a place, checked over and wired up to this and that, wheeled off for a scan was it? Then back to the limbo. She'd been hungry, asked for food, and they'd brought a tasteless sandwich. She'd been in an ambulance, rattled along invisible lanes and streets, roundabouts and traffic lights for all the world like something in *Casualty*. How had that come about?

Ah, her old friend Connie had popped in for afternoon tea. They'd been poring over the fashion adverts in *Vogue* when she, Laura, had come over a bit strange. Everything went into slow motion: she knew what she wanted to say, but she couldn't find the words; she found herself pointing at a glamorous dress in the magazine; she knew it was her favourite colour but she couldn't remember what the colours were called; her tongue wasn't working properly. 'Violent' she tried but knew it wasn't right… She'd totally lost the thread, her mind struggling to make sense of it. She'd floundered around to find another way of putting it. 'Purpose' she remembered saying, but Connie was already phoning 111 just to be on the safe side. Then the paramedics had turned up, been kind and reassuring and packed her into the ambulance with 'Better safe than sorry.'

A nurse loomed up. 'Shall we take your blood pressure then my darling?'

'Don't you "my darling" me,' she snapped. 'It's so patronising. Nobody except my husbands had the right to call me "my darling," and they're both dead.'

Laura was aware of the nurse exchanging glances with someone beyond her line of vision. She turned her head.

'Oh it's you Roger.' Bashful, her grandson's little girls came forward presenting a big bunch of roses already tumbling their petals — so like herself and her sister Joan in their pretty pink dresses.

'We picked them from your garden Great Grandma,' said Poppy, beaming.

'They prickled,' added Daisy, displaying a pinprick on her wrist.

*****

They kept her in overnight.

'You've had a TIA,' her GP told her later, 'a mini-stroke. No great harm done, let's take this as a warning.' He prescribed pills, advised her about diet and lifestyle to stave off a serious stroke.

Her sons and their bossy wives were gallivanting on their annual communal holiday to some exotic spot. When her daughter Rosemary visited, they sat comfortably sipping white wine under her late husband's favourite pear tree.

Rosemary was solicitous, nagging even, like her sisters-in-law.

'It's time you slowed down Mother. At your age, you should be taking life easy.'

'You're right dear.' She poured more wine.

'I'll tell you something darling. While I was lying there in the hospital, I saw my mother — she died when I was a little girl you know. No-one told me why one day she was there, and the next she wasn't. I thought she was stretching out a hand to pull me after her, but then I felt her hands pushing me back. And she was stuttering, trying to find the words just like I'd been a few hours earlier. She died of a massive stroke, I'm certain of it. So sad, she must have been about your age dear.'

A Case of Foul Play

Nell ran to answer the phone before it rang off. Well, in her mind she did, but her poor old legs wouldn't let her run anywhere nowadays, and she'd dozed through most of Paul O'Grady. If only she didn't wake at crack-of-dawn with those blasted birds, perhaps she wouldn't keep nodding off. Maybe Cyril was right, she should get one of those new-fangled what-d'you'm'call-its you carry around, but she'd be bound to put it down somewhere, she was getting so forgetful, and no son on earth could persuade her to keep it in her bosom like that woman on Bread. Pity they didn't have Bread on any more. The way people went about these days with those things on their ears yapping out all their private business for all the world to hear. She didn't get out much now except for Church when someone from St Edmund's fetched her. Not that she wasn't happy enough in her flat, the downstairs half of an Edwardian semi, so handy for the Health Centre if not for the shops.

Upstairs' phone shrilled ten long rings, then Les's booming voice: 'I'm afraid we're unable to take your call just now...' Nell distrusted answerphones. She picked up her knitting and zapped over to Neighbours. She liked Neighbours.

Regular as clockwork, Les and Milly came in from work at the end of Neighbours, echoing feet on the stairs, plumbing noises. Whenever their phone rang, Nell could never understand how they were always so quick at catching it after only five rings.

Milly popped in later.

'We're off on holiday next week. I'll tell Cyril, just in case.' Just in case what? As if she wasn't capable of looking after herself...

It was ever so peaceful when they'd gone, quite creepy except for that blasted answerphone, ten long rings at all hours and Cyril phoning every five minutes to make sure she was all right, not that he ever came over to Little Baddenham.

Milly's postcard was ever so nice. All that sea and sky and a palm-fringed beach staked out with half naked bodies gorging up the sun. In Nell's young days, no-one had ever exposed themselves like that and they'd never heard of skin cancer. 'Having a whale of a time. See you Sunday.'

On Sunday, Nell woke to the dawn chorus and made tea. Later, she set out the best china. They'd be wanting a nice cuppa after all that foreign muck. She eyed her lifetime of holiday souvenirs: Cromer, Clacton, and Cornwall with Reg long ago; Bruges and the Bahamas from Cyril, and the back-of-beyond from all the rest. She turned round the mug with 'Nelly' on it distastefully. She didn't like people calling her Nelly. Perhaps they'd bring a doll with a Spanish dress or a little white bull…

Nell twitched her net curtains as the taxi drew up. Its door slammed. Footsteps, the hall door, suitcases humped upstairs, then, instead of a tap on her door, that blasted answerphone. Bleeep-rhubarb-rhubarb—bleeeep-rhubarb rhubarb. It went on for ever, but even then, Milly didn't drop in. After The News, Nell put the tea things away, no good crying over wasted milk. Then she went to bed.

Despite her sleeping pill, something woke her. She sat up, fumbled for the light switch. Silence. Perhaps she'd dreamt all the shouting and sobbing, or else it was the Late Night Film. Sound didn't carry too well from upstairs' bedroom. In the morning, she heard the usual shout of 'Hurry up Milly' on the stairs.

'Is everything all right Les?' Nell called out, hiding behind her door in her housecoat and hoping they'd apologise for not popping in.

'Fine,' he said, flying past. 'Absolutely, fine!' just like in East Enders. Then the post came. Les and Milly always missed the post on weekdays. Nell examined the envelope: 'Mrs Nelly Braid,' funny writing and a foreign stamp. What could it be? But first things first. She finished dressing and went out to feed the birds. Then, with mounting excitement, she ripped open the envelope. Wrong glasses.

'My darlink Nelly,' she read. 'Here are some words only for you. I have mist you every our since we parted, I cannot leave without you. The image of your perfect breasts inflames me with desire…' Nell peered at her skinny chest, and sat down all of a flutter. Such filth! There must be some mistake. She checked the envelope and blushed furiously. Not

'Nelly Braid,' but 'Milly Brand,' and the rest was practically pornographic. The chap couldn't even spell.

Just then, Upstairs' phone rang, not ten rings, but five. Someone had picked it up, and she could have sworn they'd both gone out, not that she'd actually seen Milly. What should she do? Something very fishy indeed was happening. Best stick back the envelope anyhow. Then she'd run upstairs to check everything was all right. But her poor old legs wouldn't let her run anywhere nowadays. She creaked to the hall door and attacked Upstairs' bell. Ears agog, she heard not floorboards but the phone again. Just five rings. They were definitely in, but what would she say? Which-ever of them opened up, she mustn't let on she knew about Milly's affair. She called out up the stairs: 'Milly. Les. It's only me.' She banged the ceiling with her stick. 'There's a letter for you. I know you're in there.'

No footsteps, no reply.

Her head teemed with visions of foul play: Les lying in a pool of blood, pierced through the heart with a stiletto—but she'd heard him shouting—unless she'd nodded off and he'd come back in; Milly, bashed on the head with a blunt instrument—but no, she'd answered the phone. At least someone had. Poison, she could have taken poison, unable to bear the guilt of her adultery; or Les, in a violent fit of jealousy could have given her cyanide before sneaking out, leaving her to a lonely death. Perhaps Milly was struggling to answer the phone with her last gasp. In which case, she might still be alive, just. Nell struggled back into her own flat and dialled 999.

'But it *is* an emergency, there's a young woman dying in the flat upstairs. No of course I haven't been in, I can't manage the stairs. Anyway, it's locked.'

She rang Cyril even though he told her never to ring him at his office in Great Baddenham. 'I'm not making it up Cyril, it was the phone you see, you must come at once.'

'OK Mum, I'm on my way, but I'm sure there's nothing to worry about. Why don't you put the kettle on?'

'And could you call at the Wool Shop and get me some white gossamer 2-ply?' Cyril sounded puzzled. Miss Marple was always knitting fluffy white garments while she worked out her theory.

By the time the police arrived, Nell had looked out her magnifying glass, but it was more like The Bill really. DS This and WPC That, Suffolk Constabulary and they flashed their cards.

The PC looked vaguely familiar. Ah yes, it was Sarah Kemp's son.

'But what makes you think there's someone dead or dying up there?'

That was a teaser. She mustn't let on about the letter, not that she'd been snooping intentionally, but she didn't want to make things awkward for poor Les and Milly. And where on earth had she put the evidence anyway? It wouldn't do to leave the letter lying about for anyone to find…

'It was the phone you see, it went and they answered it and then it was the answerphone. You just break down that door, young man and you'll see I'm right.' The door gave way with an enormous crack just as the ambulance screamed up with flashing lights and Cyril close behind.

'Didn't you remember the spare key?' her son asked accusingly. How silly, in the panic, she'd clean forgotten about the emergency key.

'Is she all right?' she shouted up the stairs.

'The flat's empty Nelly,' said the WPC. 'I think you've got some explaining to do.'

The hall door opened. Les.

'What the hell's going on? What right did you have to break down my door? I'll make a complaint...'

'I think you'd better all come into my mother's flat and I'll make some tea,' Cyril was saying long-sufferingly.

'Now Mr Brand, I'm sure there will be a satisfactory explanation. But could you tell us where your wife is?'

'My wife? What's she got to do with it? She went to her sister's first thing—she's just had a baby. We had a call in the night.' Nell could feel her mouth opening and closing like a goldfish. Baby? Surely Milly hadn't said Julie was pregnant? Or had she? The Sergeant used his Walky Talky.

'That seems all right. Now, Nelly, can you tell us exactly why you—er—suspected foul play?'

'Mrs Braid to you, and Nell's my name, not Nelly,' she stalled. 'Well it's the phone you see. I knew she was in because they always pick it up after five rings except when they're out.'

It didn't sound quite right, somehow…

'Interfering old besom,' muttered Les. 'There must be a fault on the line.'

They checked the line, and the audibility of the phone, and everything was in order.

'And can you confirm, Mr Brand, that both you and your wife usually pick up the phone after five rings?'

'Of course, we have a phone in every room as well as our mobiles.'

Mobiles, that's what they were called.

'And can you account for your movements between four and five this afternoon?'

'What *is* this?' Les was getting angry again. It was dead on 4.30 when Nell had been ringing their bell and shouting. Clever of them to leave him guessing about the time he needed an alibi for. Nell longed to dazzle them all by solving the mystery. She'd never live it down if she didn't. She fiddled with the magnifying glass, hoping for inspiration.

Upstairs' phone rang, five rings. They all heard the silence. Then five more. It was ever so creepy. Nell looked round from face to face, then her eye caught a flash of movement through the window.

Settling on the roof of the bird table was a glossy starling. From its beak came the sound of five rings, then silence, and another five.

'Why, you old bugger, having us all going like that!' The starling flew off and everyone heaved sighs of relief.

'So it was a case of 'fowl play' after all,' twinkled the Sergeant. Everyone tittered. 'But it still doesn't explain why you suspected violence Mrs Braid.'

Nell suddenly remembered where she'd put the incriminating letter. It was safely tucked away down her bra. Perhaps she'd have a word with that Milly in private, but meanwhile, she'd best keep mum.

'Oh, a little bird told me,' she said airily.

The Eternal Quadrangle II
Save all your Kisses for me

Wendy smiled brightly as she swept open the long curtains. 'And how are we today Kathy? That'll be another right scorcher today.' Then she sat the old lady up, straightened her pillows and planted the breakfast tray on the cheerful counterpane. 'There's a letter come all the way from the USA. Int that nice my darling. Hev you got family over there?'

'Not that I know of.' Not like the old dear to be so vague...

'See you later, my darling.' She trundled her trolley along the corridor, humming, 'Save all your kisses for me…'

'Kathy' indeed! The cheek of these young care assistants. Katherine supposed they meant well, but it seemed so patronising. After all, everybody knew she used to be the lady of the manor. 'My darling!'

she snorted. Her late husband would have sent the girl packing for all she was a pretty little thing.

Archie's ancestors on the stairs had been prone to dying of an apoplexy and he had done likewise when his nephew Charles had explained his plans for his inheritance. There was no room for the landed gentry in the post-war world. The feudal system was as dead as the Age of Chivalry. Instead of farming, hunting and fishing and shooting, he would build a model village, complete with centrally-heated houses, schools, a surgery, shops, a library, a factory and workshops employing both men and women.

Young Frank, Katherine's erstwhile paramour, would have been frightfully keen on the concept.

'Over my dead body,' Archie had spluttered, purple in the face, and promptly collapsed muttering about damned communists, the evils of free education and how he'd leave it all to the British Legion. His existing will, remained, of course, valid.

Katherine had rattled around in Baddenham Hall for a while, but when the Higgenses retired, she took little persuading to make over the estate to the next generation, with the proviso that she retain a flat in the east wing together with a decent income. She embraced Charles and Amanda's philanthropic plans with enthusiasm. When they converted Baddenham Hall into a luxury Home for Retired Gentle Folk, they retained the East Wing for family use and when Katherine had got too frail to cope on her own, her flat was incorporated into the Home.

At last, Katherine was ready for the day and Wendy settled her into her favourite chair beside the window. Now for the letter. Ironic that her sitting-room had been Archie's old library where she'd discovered his love letters to his mistress. She held out the envelope at arm's length, fumbled for her glasses. ***Department of Women's Studies, Danforth State University, Framington, Massachusetts, USA***. What on earth was meant by 'women's studies'? She slit it open with her silver paperknife.

> *21st June 1976*
>
> *Dear Lady Marriner,*
>
> *I am a post-graduate student presently studying for a doctorate in Women's Studies. My topic is 'Sense and Sensuality in Woman Writers 1918–1939.' I first read your work in the recent anthology* **New Daughters of Eve** *(Boudicca Press, 1974) and I was so moved by the zest and spontaneity of your poetry and its obvious relevance to my subject that I moved heaven and earth to track down the whole volume.* **The Eternal Quadrangle** *is so seminal to my research that I would love to use it as a basis for my thesis, subject to copyright permissions from yourself and your publishers.*

> *Have you considered a new edition of your book? The volume would be of tremendous interest to the whole feminist movement: the heartfelt story of one woman who was brave enough to break away from the bounds of upper class convention and indulge her own sexuality, regardless of the risk of exposure, and then, when all hope of happiness was gone, when the burden of silence became too much, to bare her soul by publishing this intimate account of her sensual and emotional experiences in a dramatic bid to liberate women from the thralldom of wifehood.*

What utter codswallop!

> *I will be spending the long vacation researching in the UK and looking up my grandfather's folk. Do you know of a Harrow Farm, somewhere in Suffolk?*

Did she just!

> *It would be such a privilege to interview you in connection with my researches. Thank you for being such a wonderful poet.*
>
> *Yours very sincerely.*
>
> *Felicity Harmon (Ms)*

Katherine folded the letter, took off her reading glasses and gazed through the long window at the parched garden. In the heat-haze of that long hot summer, Capability Browne's landscaping shimmered in the periphery of her vision, obscuring the housing development; the dried up village boating lake, once the scene of laughing picnic parties; the Sports' Pavilion, once the summer house. So much was blurred around the edges now. When Sir Archie had wooed her on his return from the Great War, she had not realised the chasm of incongruity that lay between them. Though nowadays, even the memory of the crushing boredom of life with Archie was not wholly unpleasant: his bluff insensitivity; his total predictability; his stubbly chin, smelling of shaving soap, his hands of saddle wax.

*****

A figure was emerging from the Summer House, tall, slender, a dark Yeatsian lock falling across his brow. The youngster started guiltily as Katherine crossed the croquet lawn, elegant in her pale blue afternoon dress. She noticed a fleeting resemblance to the Marriner ancestors on the stairs, some wrong side of the blanket affair no doubt. He was clasping a much thumbed book—she recognised the torn Cambridge blue dust cover of *The Oxford Book of English Verse.*

'What on earth were you doing in my summerhouse young man? This is private land.'

'I know I've no right here, M'Lady, but I wasn't doing no harm. I only come here to hev a bit of privacy to read, like.'

She pushed open the summer house door, gesturing him over the threshold, and sat down on the dusty bamboo sofa while he stood awkwardly with the window behind him. She looked around: a newspaper with a headline about the marriage of the Duke of Windsor to Mrs. Wallis Simpson;

several books; matches; a few candle ends and stubs of pencils; a school exercise book; an empty ginger beer bottle or two.

'I see you have made yourself at home, young man.'

'Yes M'Lady. But…'

She smiled reassuringly.

'You don't mind?'

'Won't you sit down?' She patted the space beside her, and suddenly his features were illuminated by bright sunlight. Katherine gasped, covered her mouth in confusion: why, his resemblance to the young Archie set her pulse racing. He must be eighteen or nineteen… Her fingers tapped on her knee to calculate the years. Phew! Archie had been at sea and was seldom in Suffolk for the duration of the Great War, so the lad was unlikely to be his bastard son.

'What is your name?'

'Frank Harmon. My father has Harrow Farm.'

'Ah yes. And why are you hiding away to read poetry, Frank Harmon?'

'Because I love it M'Lady, the words set me all aglow, like. I don't want to spend my whole life tilling the soil. I want to better myself. If only I had the chance I'd quite like to go to night school, even to the university.' His eyes gleamed, then clouded over. 'Some hopes!'

And that was how it had all begun. They read poetry together, she lent him books from her husband's library. Bored with Archie's indifference and the meaninglessness of her life, her barren soul found fulfilment in cultivating Frank's intellectual powers, which blossomed under her tutelage.

Gradually, their meetings became her only reality. She showered him with gifts of books, paid for night school classes, trips to theatres and galleries. Then he began haunting both her dreams and her day time fantasies, and she was young and beautiful, a fitting mate for his virile charms. As yet, she gave no sign that would reveal the turmoil of her mind and body, nor did he reveal any feeling that was more than filial.

One day, bashful, almost tongue tied, he handed her a battered exercise book.

'That's only my scribblings,' he muttered.

His mentor read, enthralled.

'Scribblings indeed. Your poems are outstanding.'

Katherine was so impressed that she introduced her protégé to the local literary circle. When he read aloud, his voice, though countrified, was mellifluous. Before long, she suggested the côterie should set up a fund to send Frank Harmon to Cambridge to study English Literature. Given the chance, he undoubtedly had a great literary career ahead. It was their duty to send him.

'But I cannot leave you M'Lady. I love you, surely you know that?' As yet, there had been no kisses, no clandestine embraces in the summerhouse, no words of love, only their eyes connected.

'My darling,' she sighed, and the marriage of true minds ceased to be platonic.

*****

Looking back, Katherine was still amazed at what had happened. It was all very well Archie having affairs, men did, but 40 odd years ago, respectable middle aged ladies did not, unless they were totally bohemian. And she had always been taught that it was a woman's lot to lie back and think of England. Unbridled passion was hitherto totally beyond her experience, the poet Donne's 'newfoundland'. No wonder poetry had flowed out of her as never before.

Under the shadow of the imminent Second World War, the affair had been all too brief. A few delirious weeks when Archie went to Scotland for the shooting, the odd few nights when he went to London on business, or a few snatched hours in the summerhouse when he'd had local commitments. They'd danced, entwined, to their special song, 'Let's Face the Music and Dance,' continued kissing when the old windup gramophone had wound down.

The agony of separation when Frank was up at Cambridge! It had been so perfect, so unflawed, nothing had ever happened to spoil the harmony. How lucky she had been to enjoy the ardour of first love at thirty-five, an unflawed jewel, idyllic in her memory. The rarity of their meetings, the illicit nature of their love, had made their hearts grow ever fonder. The differences in their social standing had mattered not a jot.

Had their love been little more than an illusion, magnified by her yearnings and fantasies, by distance, time and rose-tinted spectacles? Or had it indeed been real?

She recalled the grey day when he'd come back to her. She was in the summerhouse, immersed in her own writing, and he had turned up out of the blue, his confidence gone, a manic intensity in his eyes.

'My tutor said my poems were second-rate adolescent rubbish.' Torn by tears, he fell into her arms.

'I felt so unworthy of you, my darling. I wanted to end it all. I would have jumped off the college tower, only my chum foiled the attempt.'

'Oh, my dear,' Katherine clung to him, stroked his head, covered him in kisses through her tears. 'You must never think you are unworthy. You have an enormous talent, your writing is first-rate, but you must know that I love you for yourself, not for your verse.'

There was no comforting him, even when she suggested that they should go away together. Although farm workers were exempt from being called up, he enlisted at once, never to return.

*****

To this day, she had never understood why she had felt compelled to publish the fruits of their love ten years after he had left her. Was it to immortalise their passion, to celebrate the triumph of love over youth and middle age? Or was it to get back at dull, dutiful, plodding Archie by telling the whole world that a handsome young Adonis had chosen to love her, yes her, past her best and middle-aged, not just for her mind, but for her body? Or was it just to make Archie notice her? Was it some kind of catharsis, an attempt to purge the secret guilt?

If she had not nurtured Frank's undoubted talent, he would not have suffered the ultimate despair that led to what amounted to his self-destruction. And was it to protect his anonymity that she had included some of his poems, intermixed with her own outpourings of passion, without attributing them to her lost young love?

The publication of Katherine's book, The Eternal Quadrangle, in 1949 had whirl-winded her into glorious, if brief, fame, notoriety even. She'd mulled it all over in her mind so much that, for the life her, she could no longer distinguish between her motivation in the preceding decade, and that which she had superimposed on her memories in the long succeeding years.

How invigorating it had all been! Hot stuff! Her book was in its old place, shrouding her dead lover's last letter from the front, the letter protesting that they could never be together because of the disgrace that would fall upon her.

'Coffee or tea Kathy?' Wendy disturbed her revery. 'Or would you prefer a cold drink, seeing as it's so hot?'

'I'd like you to bring my writing case, Wendy.'

'Why you're miles away, my darling, it must be the weather.'

'And please do not tell my nephew about the letters. There's a good girl.'

'You can trust me, my darling,' Wendy winked as she put the drink on the bed table.

That's Little Baddenham

Dear Miss Harmon,

I do not think an interview would help with your research. I suggest you confine your studies to the text. I am an old lady now, and such a meeting would bring back memories that are best left forgotten.

> *I am sure you are familiar with the works of John Keats. Might I refer you to the sentiments expressed in his 'Ode on a Grecian Urn'? I quote the most pertinent lines. They might help to explain my own small work and my reticence about it.*

> She cannot fade, though thou hast not thy bliss,
> For ever wilt thou love, and she be fair!...
> When old age shall this generation waste,
> Thou shalt remain, in midst of other woe…
> Beauty is truth, truth beauty — that is all
> Ye know on earth, and all ye need to know.

Yours sincerely,

Katherine Marriner

By the time Wendy returned to escort the old lady to lunch, Kathie was dead, just slipped away peacefully in her chair, poor old thing. She'd finished her letter, and had been scribbling a few words on a new sheet. Seeing as the envelope was addressed, but unsealed, Wendy popped in both sheets and posted it.

Seek not to wake the sleeping dead,
But let their secrets lie.
Exposure to the cruel air
Can only petrify.

Exposure to the cruel air
Can tarnish precious stones.
Seek not to mar those memories
Of kaleidoscopic tones…

The Happening

I really and truly don't know what happened that night, Mirabel, honest to God I don't. There were these flashing lights, I do remember that, and the music was so loud you couldn't hardly think and everyone was dancing as if they'd never stop. The air was thick with I'm not quite sure what, and as for the booze, well I had hully more than what I was used to. Since Rehab with Alcoholics Anonymous, my Dad had allus been a bit strict about what us kids had to drink.

I were engaged, so I felt a bit out of it actually. Joe, being so much older than me, didn't hold with raves, and I must say I come to agree with him after that particular Happening, but he'd been OK about me going on my own. After all, it was my sister's Hen Night. We all had a few Babychams — nothing stronger I swear — in between bopping about with the gals. I sat down for a bit beside my cousin Liz who drone on and on about her morning sickness. I couldn't hardly hear her above the noise. Then this boy grab my hand for a dance. I prefer older men myself, and he were all over me, breathing beery fumes in my face, even touching me up. I had a bit of trouble pushing him off I can tell you, Mirabel. By the end of the night I was slightly fuddled. Someone must of spiked my drink, perhaps slipped me LSD, I just don't know.

No, not too much off Mirabel, just below the ears.

Anyways, when I woke up, I was safe at home in my own bed feeling a bit mazy. If that was a hangover I didn't want another and the alarm clock was drumming in my head. To crown it all, I was just in the middle of this mind-blowing dream — the kind when you long to go back to sleep so you can find out what happen next.

There was this angel gawping at me, with floaty wings, all in white, gleaming and spot-lit for all the world like Elvis. A backing group was softly singing 'Marie's the Name, His Latest Flame.'

'Hi Marie,' he say, 'you gonna have a baby.' I felt all shook up at the sound of his voice, I can tell you Mirabel.

'Who me?' I yell, aghast. 'That's not possible, my Joe, he don't believe in sex before marriage. You must be hully crazed.'

'Hold you hard gal, that's gonna be a very special baby. God's the father, and your son's gonna save the world. God chose you specially to be his mother, if that's OK by you.'

Of course we was all going to save the world back in the sixties, weren't we? What with waking up all of a sudden, I never found out whether I agreed. Or not. The Raven with copper highlights please, Mirabel.

Anyways, when I tell Liz I was late and feeling slightly sick in the mornings, she rush me off to the doctor.

'But I can't be pregnant,' I tell him. 'I've never slept with no-one in my whole life.'

The Quack winked knowingly at me.

'Come now, are you quite certain?' Then I remembered the hen night and the drunken stupor and I weren't sure at all. Perhaps I'd been taken advantage of. My sister, she weren't none the wiser.

But how to account for it to Mum and Joe? I know it were the swinging sixties when people slept around. Lots of my friends had to get married and being an unmarried mother wasn't as shameful as it had been, but Little Baddenham was a right hotbed of gossip. Mum, hearing me throwing up, she soon guessed.

'You'll just have to put forward the wedding, gal,' she say, putting her finger to her mouth with a knowing look, 'and make out it were a honeymoon baby and a bit prem. Best not tell your Dad. Nor your Joe.'

But I had to tell Joe, or he'd never forgive me. But would he still want to marry me? My Joe were a bit old-fashioned, and deeply religious, and I loved him too much to hurt him like that. Besides, I was beginning to show. He'd already commented on my sudden fancy for cherryade. Well, I'd never ever seen Joe so angry before, and I never heard him use them names he call me.

'If you think I'm going to marry you when you're carrying someone else's brat you can think again, you whore.'

Well, I tried to explain about the angel, and how it was God's will and everything would be all right, but it dint make much sense somehow. The story dint go down too well, I can tell you, Mirabel, but what else could I say? If only the angel could have a word with Joe, he might believe me. But I dint know how to get hold of the angel. It wasn't as if he'd given me his phone number. Perhaps if I slip whatever it was I'd been given into Joe's tea, he might see the angel too, but I had no idea how to set this up. I even writ to Elvis. Perhaps if I went to church a bit more and prayed harder… Joe was in a right black mood for days. He even cancelled the caterers, but suddenly all was well.

'That's OK my darling,' he say tenderly, 'I now know you're telling the truth.'

'How?' I say, cuddling into him as far as my bump would allow.

'Shall we say a special messenger?' he said airily, and we were married immediately.

When I went into labour, Joe, he were working away — Dads wasn't expected to dance attendance and hold your hand in the delivery ward in them days.

When they said I had a daughter, I were gobsmacked. The story of the angel wouldn't hold water if the baby was a girl… I must of looked disappointed. 'Better luck next time eh? There's another one inside,' grinned the nurse.

Twins! I hadn't been expecting twins. I was a bit tired, but my mind were in a whirl. There were no way I could get away with having two babies, not after I'd told Joe what the angel had said about a special boy. Joe must never know. Best not ask me how I wangled it, but by the time Joe turn up, I was lying there cradling my little boy, and some poor foreign woman who'd lost her baby had got my daughter. I pinned a message on her woolly white shawl. 'Her name is Marie.'

Josh were a lovely baby, a lovely little boy, but he never quite fit in with the other kids at school. He were always restless, a rainbow dreamer, always looking for something, or someone. Sometimes I wondered if it was the twin thing—not that he'd ever known he had a twin sister—I'd made sure of that you may be sure, Mirabel. You know how they say you still feel pain in a limb that's been amputated? I suppose it's a bit like that.

And he were so intense, always throwing himself into some cause or other, championing the underdog, laying down the law. He even stood up to the headmaster once when he thought some boy had been punished unfairly. Then he went off to Uni, grew a long beard and hair, wore sandals and bare feet, ever so untidy if you ask me. If there was a demo, he were right there in London, outside No 10, shouting and waving banners on TV but no violence—he never lift a finger to hurt man or beast. Dint seem to have no time for girlfriends. No, he wasn't one of them neither.

Anyways, after Uni he went travelling, you know how they do. Hardly heard from him for months, just the odd postcard from places I couldn't pronounce but you heard about in the news as being hotbeds of corruption. Then one day Josh writ and say he'd met this girl. 'We're soulmates,' he say. 'We're the same person.' Must be a special girl I thought to myself—Joe was long since dead by then.

Then he rang from the airport. 'We're on our way home!'

I sat fretting in the window expecting them on every bus. Then there they were, weighed down by back packs, striding along our road, hand in hand. Even from that distance I could see they was hully wrapped up in each other. There was a radiance about them somehow.

I was on the doorstep to meet them. Josh gave me a bear hug.

'Hi Mum. This is Maddy.'

'Hi there,' she say, in a soft accent I couldn't quite place. She was holding out her hand to me, but blow me, you could of knocked me down with a feather, for she was the spitten image of me when I was young.

'My first name is Marie,' she was saying, 'but that son of yours he is always calling me by my middle name so's not to confuse his two best girls. Says he!'

That were a bloomin' rum old do!

Thanks Mirabel, a new hairdo always perk you up.

Keep the change.

The Copper Beech

It had to go, the glorious copper beech, so long a ritual point in her daily landscape, so much in harmony with the Suffolk-pink cottage it guarded.

Every morning, the tree was there when Connie let the cat out, swathed in whatever light the season held. Every night, it reached up towards the moon or scudding clouds as she called the cat in.

Standing at the kitchen sink, Connie strove desolately to etch the image of the tree in her brain before its final desecration. She could hardly make out the time, as her tears dripped onto her glasses, but the clock ticked on, counting down the seconds towards noon when the tree fellers were due.

How could she possibly live on without the tree of her life?

Snapshots, undimmed by intervening years and failing sight, flashed through her consciousness. Beneath the tree: the newlyweds relaxing on striped deckchairs; a succession of cats, babies, *al fresco* meals for themselves, the children, the grand-children. She saw: an aging Bill, puffing at his meerschaum, chopping logs in his threadbare gardening clothes; a cat, washing disdainfully, refusing to come down from the tree-house in fear of the vet. Hammocks, swings and Tarzan ropes swung from the branches where pigeons still indulged in noisy fore-play and cooed relentlessly through the long summer days.

Connie constantly revelled in the many-textured rustling of leaves in the wind or underfoot. Each autumn, she would bring an armful of twigs into the house before they shed their copper leaves. Each summer, once the gas fire became redundant, she would gather more to decorate the inglenook.

Hanging up the tea towel, Connie went into the garden, a perfect September morning with a hint of autumn. Her feet crunkled on the beech mast, once laboriously threaded into necklaces, proudly offered as gifts but too prickly to wear. She sat down on her old green chair under the canopy of the tree. Flossie stopped scratching the silvery bark and leapt onto her lap, circling, purring, kneading, unaware of her predecessors buried there.

Did the tree pre-date the cottage? How many generations had enjoyed it? How many mothers had sung, 'and the leaf was on the twig, and the twig was on the branch…'?

Now, it had to go, the copper beech had to go: its roots were undermining the foundations, cracking walls and floors. For a time, its fate had hung in the balance, hotly debated by conflicting conservation bodies, listed timber-framed cottage *versus* ancient tree, both protected species, and no-one could be sure whether the root damage was irreparable.

Her son had accused her of gross sentimentality: her daughter had told her not to be such a fuss-pot. Only her old friend, Laura Cruickshank, had understood her anguish. The one remaining decision was hers alone: to witness the death throes of the tree was impossible; to escape for the day, as Laura suggested, and return to that gaping hole in the landscape, was equally unbearable.

In the end, Connie decided to stay and witness the execution. Her presence might sooth the passing of the great tree, whose ent-like cries had ridden so many storms. So majestic a being must surely be sentient. But the tree-fellers, arriving only ten minutes late, after quantities of tea and unloading of gear, pronounced that they couldn't guarantee her safety if she remained on the premises during the operation.

'Only a precaution,' reassured the foreman.

'Better safe than sorry,' grinned his mate.

The boy had a final slurp at the dregs of sugary tea.

So Connie took herself off to the Dancing Goat for lunch, thence to St Edmund's churchyard where Flossie emerged from behind a gravestone, flaunted a dead blackbird, then slunk off. To a background of shrieking chain saws, she tidied Bill's grave, then took sanctuary inside the church. The heavy oak door reduced the volume, but she could still hear the banshee screech. On the lectern, the bible was open at Isaiah 44, the passage about the use of trees.

> Half of the wood he burns in the fire; over it
> he prepares his meal, he roasts his meat and
> eats his fill. He also warms himself and
> says, 'Ah ha! I am warm; I see the fire. From
> the rest he makes a god, his idol; he bows
> down to it and worships. He prays to it and
> says, 'Save me! You are my god!'

The whining blade continued. Surely it must be nearly over. Connie felt she could add a thing or two to the prophet's list of utilities. She rather thought her sympathies fell with the heathen idolaters. She glanced up at the church roof. A carved angel seemed to be smiling down on her. It winked its wooden eye...

At last, blessed silence, and with it, a sense of release. The church clock struck three. Surely it was safe to go home now. Connie crossed Market Hill, lowering her eyes as she approached her cottage against the inevitable hole in the skyline with a degree of equanimity. The men were loading their truck. The boy was already feeding the shredder with small branches and twigs, the burnished leaves still glinting as they met their end.

'You'll find it a lot lighter,' smiled the foreman.

'You'll be as safe as houses now,' guffawed the mate.

They led her round the cottage and into the back garden. The remains of the trunk, sawed into manageable lengths, lay elephantine on the ground; tentacles of roots spread above an immense crater, already alive with dispossessed insects and worms. The pecking birds dispersed with a rush of wings as Flossie leapt in, extracted a long worm which she tossed up and down, delighted with its wiggling. A draggled nest or two adorned the lawn. No bones, Connie couldn't see any feline skulls.

'What do you want us to do with the remains? We can take them away, or chop them into logs. We can get you a good price for the logs…'

It reminded her of the vet asking if she wanted a departed cat to be incinerated.

She hadn't really thought beyond the execution, but now the prophet Isaiah guided her.

'I won't have you taking anything away,' she pronounced. 'I'd appreciate it if you could make logs from the bigger branches. You can put them in the log store at the side of the house. But leave the trunk.'

She caught the men looking at each other meaningfully. 'Batty old thing,' their eyes said.

'Are you sure, my dear?' said the foreman.

'You haven't got an open fire,' said the mate.

'Quite sure.'

While the shredder churned the twigs into mulch, Connie was already looking up builders in the Yellow Pages. She'd open up the chimney, have a real log fire, make toast with a toasting fork, roast chestnuts and potatoes when the family came for Christmas…

*****

Autumn, winter, spring, ambled by, and the desolate space was no longer desolate. It was May, and the sun beamed freely down on new growth where the desert had been. Connie, screened by a wide straw hat, was sitting knitting on the rustic seat the local carpenter had knocked up for her. 'Make me a memory seat for my declining years' she'd asked. Beside her, Flossie and her kittens were rampaging at their new scratching post, the envy of the neighbourhood. The water feature, constructed where the crater had been, trickled soothingly, its raw edges mellowing as the plants thrived. Connie glanced lovingly at the potted infant saplings. The discovery of the tiny nuts sprouting bold green shoots had been a significant moment. She watered them from the new pond, nurtured them with their parental mulch. One day, she'd plant one far away from the cottage. The rest she'd give to family, friends and the church plant sale.

She'd donated branches to a wood turner she'd encountered at the Gala craft fair. At Laura's suggestion, she'd commissioned a massive creation from a woodcarver.

Today the sculpture was coming and she was bubbling with anticipation. The spirit of the tree would live on, and all was right with the world.

THE CRUICKSHANK CHRONICLES V
A GRAVE MISTAKE

Before she'd had the children, Avril Cruickshank had been practice manager at Great Baddenham Surgery. Subsequently, Julian's large income had allowed her to devote her life to supporting the community. She played a prominent role on the town council and also in charitable fund-raising. When these activities palled, she put herself forward for the District Council and served on the Planning Committee.

One day, an Application came in from the Evergreen Housing Association relating to Orchard Place, Little Baddenham, her mother-in-law Laura's family home. Consent was sought for: Phase One — Change of Use of existing property to a Care Home; Phase Two — development of the grounds as a complex of Sheltered Lodges.

Avril was almost foaming at the mouth. Excavations would undoubtedly reveal the dark family secret of buried bones in the orchard. She phoned her husband, although he didn't like to be interrupted in Chambers where he might be in the midst of some complex and confidential legal consultation.

'What?' Julian exploded. 'Over my dead body!'

Now Avril was well aware that the townsfolk of Little Baddenham had been clamouring for such a facility in the light of an aging community and the cut back in bus services, but she vowed to move heaven and earth to withhold the permission, pointing out a more practical location adjoining the Sports' Field. In spite of her campaign, her views were overridden by the local worthies who had earmarked the Sports' Centre site for a much needed Youth Facility.

Julian, she knew, had thoroughly investigated the legality of burying his father in the orchard, but if the bones were discovered after thirty-five years, embarrassing questions would be asked that would prejudice his position and the family's credibility. Luckily, their son Roger worked in Building Regulations.

'Roger,' she decreed, 'you must do everything in your power to string matters out as long as you can. We can't afford a hint of scandal to prejudice your father's chances of being appointed judge, it's now or never…'

'Why?' Then Avril remembered that the next generation had never been told about the orchard burial and explained.

They all agreed that Julian's mother, Laura, should remain unaware of the machinations as long as possible. There was no need to upset her further. Avril had long suspected that Laura was still tortured by guilt. Perhaps she'd been too fazed by Guy's death to take in that his burial in the orchard had in fact been perfectly above board. Now she'd been widowed for the second time, but Geoff's funeral had been with bells, smells and benefit of clergy.

'Laura is a bit confused after her second stroke, so we can't rely on her not coming out with the grisly truth,' said Avril.

'I wouldn't count on it,' said Roger's wife, Clare. 'She's much shrewder than you give her credit for, and she's raring to be more independent. She's bound to find out some time.'

Of course, thought Avril, nowadays, Greenfield burials were commonplace, but it really wouldn't do for the world at large to discover that the Cruickshanks, pillars of the community and above reproach, had been harbouring a dark secret for thirty odd years. If it ever got out, they'd become a laughing stock…

*****

The Chief Executive of Evergreen Retirement Homes grew increasingly exasperated by the delays.

'We need the place to become operational to get some return from our investment.'

Diggins and Son, builders, were disgruntled because they'd put other operations on hold.

'Contract jobs like this don't grow on trees, son, what with the recession,' said Nick Diggins.

'We shouldn't have moved to Little Baddenham before there were jobs to go to,' said Robby Ray, Manager Designate, to his wife Norma, Head of Care Designate.

'We need our Care Home now,' demanded the townsfolk, waving banners outside the Council offices. 'What's stopping them at least revamping the old house to be going on with?'

In the end, Avril's machinations failed, but at least Julian had been promoted to judge.

*****

Apart from Laura, who was suffering from a tummy bug, the Cruickshanks, *en masse*, attended the Official Opening of Orchard Place Retirement Complex together with the local worthies and relatives of the newly ensconced clients of the now gleaming old house. Rosie's friends were there, Stella and Louise, with her aged mother, Jean was it? There were speeches, cream teas in the garden, an exhibition showing the future development for which the local MP laid the foundation stone.

'It looks as if we're going to get away with it Julian, touch wood.' Avril downsized her voice in an attempt to whisper. Her eyes involuntarily strayed towards The Spot in the orchard where a couple were gesticulating wildly to their grown-up children. They looked vaguely familiar, Rosie and Ian seemed to know them... Ah yes, the couple who'd bought the place. Intrigued, Avril seized Julian's arm and wandered over. Good heavens, where were the all concealing paving slabs? Perhaps this couple knew all and were keeping it to themselves…

'Hi!' said the man. 'We're indulging in a spot of nostalgia, seeing the old place for the last time before the bulldozers move in. We're the recent owners,' he explained. Avril refrained from commenting on the coincidence of two sets of previous occupants meeting. 'Sold up a couple of years ago, needs must once we'd got our large family off our hands. Couldn't afford to do much to the house, let the grounds run riot. Look Si, that's where we had the swing.'

'And that's where we had the tree house,' said one of the girls pointing up at the pear tree where a solitary plank hung crazily.

'Only tree in the whole orchard with branches that would support the structure,' said the father. 'Had to dig up some antediluvian paving slabs in case of accidents. Never understood why anyone was fool enough to put a patio on the edge of an orchard. We turned it over to Veg.'

'I've never seen a vegetable patch so fertile,' said the wife. 'Our produce won no end of prizes in The Flower Show and as for those roses on that arch thingy… The locals weren't best pleased and no-one could account for it.'

Avril could, but she kept her peace. She found herself holding her breath and exhaled slowly. The man would have said if he'd found bones, but then the brothers had dug the regulation six feet down. Perhaps the bulldozers wouldn't dig that far…

'Nice to meet you,' Mr er?' she smiled graciously, speaking in her best District Councillor voice.

'Newton, Bob Newton. And this is Trish.' He held out his hand to be shaken.

'It must have been a happy home.' It certainly had been in Laura and Guy's time, with plenty of space for the brothers to run around. Perhaps she and Julian should have bought it from Laura when she downsized, then there would have been no danger of discovery…

*****

The Cruickshank brothers and their wives had recently returned from a world cruise in celebration of some significant birthdays and retirements. One Saturday, Avril, failing to find her sister-in-law Rosie at The Treasure Trove, popped into The Crown in Little Baddenham where she knew the ladies of the town assembled for coffee and gossip. She glanced around. No Rosie.

She chose a large scrubbed-pine table, ordered and sat back in solitary splendour to enjoy the venerable ambience. The place was humming. She'd idly picked up a newspaper from the display stand as she came in.

THE NURSING HOME MURDER
Bulldozers excavating the foundations of Phase Two of Orchard Place Retirement Complex in Little Baddenham uncovered bones thought to be human…

Avril caught her breath, raised her hand to check her shades were in place, relaxed a little when she noticed the paper was considerably out of date.

'Excuse me,' a voice was saying, 'are these chairs taken?'

The hotel was so busy, Avril could hardly refuse and graciously moved aside to a tiny table. Four middle aged women sat down and tried to catch the eye of the waitress. The place had gone downhill since she and Laura had been regulars.

'It were my husband that went down into the hole and inspected them bones,' said a plump woman, pointing at the headline in Avril's East Anglian. 'His grandfather were the sexton, and he wondered if the corpse had been some centuries-old suicide that couldn't be buried in the churchyard. Nick had half a mind to say nothing and just put them back.'

The waitress trotted up, pad in hand.

'Good morning Mrs Diggins, what can I get you ladies?' After lengthy discussion, the order was agreed.

'That would have been quite wrong Maureen,' retorted the woman with smartly dyed hair.

'Too right Mirabel,' said the one with glasses. 'My daughter what works in accounts say them big brass from Evergreen and Robby Ray was ever so upset, complained that calling in the police would put them out of business after all that hassle with Planning Permission and such like.'

'That's true for Nick's business and all,' said Mrs Diggins.

'But they done the right thing in the end,' said the woman with faded red hair. 'My son's a policeman, and he should know.'

'Is that so Sarah?' said the one with glasses. The waitress came with the coffees and interrupted the flow.

'They had to treat the death as suspicious, called in the Coroner, the pathologist, the lot,' resumed

Sarah. 'They reckon the bones weren't ancient at all, they'd been there about thirty years and no sign of foul play.'

'My neighbour Stella's keen on archaeology. She'd been hoping for Anglo-Saxon remains and treasure,' said the one with glasses.

'Trish Newton what lived there until Evergreen bought it up tell me they DNA'd her and Bob, most put out she was. You hear all sorts in the salon.'

'I should think so too, Mirabel. And then the police searched for Missing Persons and none to be found. They must have suspected murder with all that carrying on, isn't that right Sara? And there was some problem about tracking down the family before them. Crook was it? They were all off gallivanting round the world, seemingly.'

Avril's instinct was to escape before anyone recognised her, but calling for her bill would only draw attention to herself.

'Morning Norma,' said Mrs Diggins to a newcomer, 'we're nearly done.' Avril froze. Laura's 'treasure' would be bound to recognise her. She checked her shades.

'Wait till I tell you who's just moved into Orchard Place? I didn't recognise the name, she'd always got a lot of gumption that one, went and got married again.' Her cronies looked blank.

'Go on Norma, tells us all.'

'Old Mrs Crookwhatever what I used to work for before I went into caring.'

Avril started. Good heavens, this was the first she had heard of the move, Laura was a wily old thing. The whole family had been trying for years to persuade her to go into sheltered accommodation, particularly after her second stroke, but, stubborn as she was, she'd taken any such suggestion as an affront to her dignity and her ability to look after herself. Perhaps Rosie had managed to persuade her.

'You don't say,' said Mirabel.

'I have a feeling all this corpse stuff wasn't new to her,' said Norma. When I told her, her old eyes glazed up like a hare caught in the headlights. I bet she could tell us a thing or two...'

Avril collected herself and her belongings, paid her bill, and strode off to the car park. Before driving off in search of Laura, she texted the siblings. They were on their way.

*****

Avril negotiated the security system of Orchard Place Care Home. At least the old entrance hall retained some of its former dignity.

'Your mother-in-law has put her name down for the first Lodge to become available,' said the receptionist, 'but she insisted on moving in immediately. Norma, our Head of Care, agreed. You'll find she's a bit agitated.'

Avril was curious. Laura looked tiny, sitting in a recliner chair in one half of the former kitchen. On the wall, hung a large picture of the pear tree in full bloom. Her niece Miranda's florid signature leapt out of the orchard. Tony's girl was making quite a name for herself in the art world.

'Avril my dear, how good of you to call. I was beginning to think your cruise ship had gone down like the Titanic. I don't get much news here...'

Avril bent to kiss her. Nothing wrong with her memory then.

'I'm sure your moving in here was a wise choice, Laura, but I'm surprised you didn't wait till we all got back. I don't know what Rosie was thinking off…'

'Rosemary had nothing to do with it, she was off in South America buying more stock for The Treasure Trove.'

'Why the rush then?'

'Call me a silly old woman if you like…'

'You may be old Mother, but I've never thought of you as silly,' said Julian, blustering into the room with Rosie behind him. They both bent to kiss Laura.

'Ian and I have been time-tripping at Kentwell Hall since we got home, I haven't a clue what's been going on.'

Laura looked uncomfortable, fumbled around for a tissue, dabbed it to her eyes.

'Well, you see, my dears, it's poor Guy's bones. Someone had to keep an eye on them. Think of the trouble we'd be in if it all came to light. Our illegal and immoral action has been haunting me for years.'

'But Mother…' they chorused. Rosie was fiddling with her phone. Julian was scratching his bald patch when the door opened and Tony swept in.

'Hi folks,' sorry I'm late.' He bent to kiss his mother.

'But me no buts, but hear me out,' Laura continued. 'All the time I could talk to Guy, right there under the pear tree,' she gestured towards the building site, the area cordoned off with police tape, 'I was content. Guy was happy when I married Geoff, I know it. But then Geoff died, it was a judgement on me for being so deceitful, and the second stroke as well, and now it's all coming to light I'm being punished, we'll all be punished, you just wait and see... Poor Guy, he should have been buried in Holy Ground like Geoff... it's been haunting me for years...'

Avril had never known Laura to be hysterical. Rosie was hugging her, making soothing noises.

'But Laura...' Avril felt it incumbent upon her to take charge of the situation, the others were flapping around like headless chicken. 'Surely you knew?'

'Knew what?'

'We did nothing illegal. Do you honestly think Julian would have countenanced anything illegal? Even in view of his father's dying wishes?'

Poor old Laura was weeping openly now.

'Or in breach of health and safety?' Avril continued.

'There are rules about distances from water courses,' added Julian, 'and we jolly well obeyed them.' Laura looked up, removed her tear-stained glasses, and fixed her faded blue eyes on them all in turn.

'Then why on earth didn't you tell me at the time? I've been plagued with agonies of guilt for years — suffering I could have been spared if only you'd been honest. Was it a conspiracy of silence?'

No-one spoke, then they were all protesting at once.

'I didn't know anything about legalities let alone illegalities at the time,' said Rosie. 'You all thought I was too young to understand.'

'We didn't want to worry you, Mother, did we Tony?' said Julian.

'But why? Why all the secrecy? All the lies? Why did we go through that pantomime of telling everyone there had been a private cremation?'

'Come off it Mother, we didn't actually lie, you know,' said Julian.

'How hypocritical can you get?' said Rosie. 'I suppose you all let it be assumed. Typical lawyer, manipulating the truth in order to get a verdict.'

Avril had never seen Julian so enraged. Laura was looking steely eyed.

'But why?'

'I'll tell you why,' said Tony vehemently. 'It's because we Cruicshanks are a bunch of stuck-up, self-satisfied conventionalists who can't abide a hint of anything outré. We're two faced and dishonest. Back then, we were all on tenterhooks in case Barbara blurted out the truth and offended the world and his wife. Do you remember that bit in Under Milk Wood? "What'll the neighbours?..." Bugger the neighbours! My wife Barbara, who is stuck in a parents' meeting by the way, is honest, so's Rosie, but I'm ashamed of belonging to this family and all its hypocrisy.'

Everyone shuffled around uncomfortably with mutterings of 'how could you, Tony…'

Then Laura gathered up her dignity and addressed them.

'Can someone tell me why you kept me in the dark?'

'We all thought you knew,' said Julian.

'You were totally traumatised by Guy's death, we didn't want to add to your sufferings by dwelling on the matter,' said Avril.

'It just wasn't something we talked about,' said Tony.

'I suppose it all boils down to that typically British Stiff Upper Lip,' said Rosie. 'It's much derided abroad.'

Laura spoke.

'How could you? And all for the sake of losing face.'

There was a long silence, then Laura reached out to pick up the phone.

'No Mother, you mustn't...' said Julian grabbing her arm, but she jerked her hand free then pressed a number three times.

'Police please. I have information relating to the bones found at Orchard Place...'

Laura looked suddenly older, drained.

'Julian, I can hardly ask a dishonourable man to do the honours, but now we're all ready to come clean I think we all need a stiff drink. That's what Guy would have wanted, I know it.'

ABOUT THE AUTHOR

Ann Elliott has a degree in English. She entered two short stories in a Children's Newspaper competition at the tender the age of ten, published in student magazines, wrote concert reviews for regional newspapers and started writing seriously some twenty five years ago.

Earlier versions of some of the stories in *That's Little Baddenham* appeared in two anthologies: Wensum Wordsmiths: *Mischief and Mayhem. Norwich 1798* (1998), and *Time and Time Again* (2000) 'Over the Top' was in the top five entries in the 2009 ITV 'This Morning' short story competition.

In 2012 she published *Too Many Tenors,* a novel about the shenanigans among choral singers.

She is currently working on *Those Pollok Girls*, a two generation family saga based loosely on early twentieth century family history.

Ann has spent most of her adult life in East Anglia, but from time to time needs to indulge her passion for rugged hills, rock strewn rivers, cliff lined coasts and 'her' Sussex Downs.

She has always sung in choirs and loves early and folk music. She enjoys theatre, galleries, historic buildings, the countryside, walking, wild flowers and dogs and cats.

Rufus, the toy poodle, who features in two of the stories has passed on to the Happy Hunting Ground in the sky.

Too Many Tenors, debut novel by Ann Elliott

'Dateline, the in thing back in 1979, couldn't have selected a

more perfectly matched couple, or so we thought...

Hot-foot from honeymoon, Alison and Rick settle in Yarchester, where Rick sings in the Cathedral Choir. With their shared love of music, they expect perfect harmony, but Alison finds singing in choirs is not entirely sweet. Relationships founder under the stress of philanderings, musical rivalry and the cathedral anti-social hours. The St Cecilia's Singers suffer life-threatening defections. Humour and heartache go hand in hand as Alison strives to preserve her marriage.

In true Trollopian tradition, Yarchester Cathedral, its Close, Choir and school, is ever present. The two choirs are not just an arena for the shennanigens among the singers: the conflict between personal and public loyalty is pivotal. Should family or art come first?

'An unusually themed novel with a core of central characters linked by choral music, back biting and complicated love lives. Ms Elliott illustrates a clear understanding of the bewilderment, pain and desperation which can occur when someone is let down and betrayed by those they trust most.'

'I enjoyed the sparse wittiness in the dialogue.'

'Full of texture, just enough political context to support the time-line, and a wicked almost-twist at the end. You don't have to like choral music to enjoy what is a very well written, tender, and at times laugh-out-loud funny saga.'

'There is a sort of wit and lack of earnestness, which shows in nick-names like' Sweet Basil, Gloria in Excelsis *and* My Cat Jeoffrey, *also the chapter headings, quotations from the text of compositions in honour of St Cecilia, patron saint of music.*

If you have enjoyed **That's Little Baddenham**, please recommend it to your friends and take a few minutes to review it on Amazon or Goodreads.

https://www.facebook.com/anntelliottauthor/
http://anntelliott@wixsite.com

Made in the USA
Columbia, SC
16 October 2017